I0819114

ALSO BY TOMÁS Q. MORÍN

POETRY

Machete

Patient Zero

A Larger Country

NONFICTION

Where Are You From: Letters to My Son

Let Me Count the Ways

AS EDITOR

Coming Close: Forty Essays on Philip Levine

AS TRANSLATOR

The Heights of Macchu Picchu by Pablo Neruda

CAT LOVE

CAT LOVE

A Novel

♥

TOMÁS Q. MORÍN

PANTHEON BOOKS · NEW YORK

FIRST HARDCOVER EDITION
PUBLISHED BY PANTHEON BOOKS 2026

Published by Pantheon Books, a division of Penguin Random House LLC, 1745 Broadway, New York, NY 10019.

Library of Congress Cataloging-in-Publication Data
Names: Morín, Tomás Q., author.
Title: Cat love / Tomás Q. Morín.
Description: First hardcover edition. | New York : Pantheon Books, 2026. |
Identifiers: LCCN 2025033930 (print) | LCCN 2025033931 (ebook) |
ISBN 9780593702048 hardcover | ISBN 9780593702055 ebook
Subjects: LCGFT: Animal fiction | Novels | Fiction
Classification: LCC PS3613.O7542 C38 2026 (print) |
LCC PS3613.O7542 (ebook)
LC record available at https://lccn.loc.gov/2025033930
LC ebook record available at https://lccn.loc.gov/2025033931

penguinrandomhouse.com | pantheonbooks.com

Printed in the United States of America
1st Printing

The authorized representative in the EU for product safety and compliance is Penguin Random House Ireland, Morrison Chambers, 32 Nassau Street, Dublin D02 YH68, Ireland, https://eu-contact.penguin.ie.

For Lindsey Anne Lou Sticktail Morín
I miss you, baby girl

The future ain't what it used to be.

—YOGI BERRA

CAT LOVE

EMOTIONAL STATISTICS

"In the field of study best known as emotional statistics, the word "maybe" is a term of art . . . is the language of the wanted and the language of the one doing the wanting . . ."

—Charles Yu, "32.05864991%"

Course Description

This ten-day course will emphasize feeling and the feeling process, including pre-feeling and emotional revision. Students will take daily quizzes in response to the Schrödinger's cat experiment, as well as read and react to the feelings of classmates in order to improve emotional competency. Emotions are a process, not an event, and the best way to improve is to feel often and deeply. All of this takes time and work.

Requirements

PPE (Personal Protective Equipment: laboratory coat, gloves, safety glasses, appropriate footwear (no open-toed shoes), fit-tested respirator, and good-luck charm.

What our students are saying . . .

"This was the best emotional experience I've ever had! Thank you so much! You're the best!"

—Nina L.

“I thank you for the program. With my certificate I am now off my deferred sentence.”

—Vic Z.

“I am forty-eight years of age and learned a great deal. Not only was this a great refresher course, but it has opened up a whole new career path for me. I am very pleased.”

—Misha P.

NB: Please do not bring a cat. The cat, box, and vial of poison are provided by the Institute.

Call me . . . call me whatever you like. I've had many names over the years. Did you think I was going to say Ishmael? Or actually tell you my real name? Not today. Maybe not tomorrow, either. I bet you're wondering how a cat knows about *Moby-Dick*. Especially the tortoiseshell cat sealed in the box in this lab.

This box doesn't define my existence, you know. Although, if you already knew that, you could've tested out of this class and not had to take it. But you didn't, and so here we are, under these awful lights. You, in your white coats and masks, taking notes, sitting in a circle and staring at me inside this glass box.

I can see the food on your breath and taste the fear in your tapping shoes. I can even see the ridiculous poster on the wall behind me of a penguin and polar bear embracing above the words "An Eye for an Eye Makes the World Go Blind." You think that I can't see you, that I can only see my reflection. Well, that just shows how much you know about seeing.

Ahab had a problem with seeing, too. Okay, I confess that I read the book. Maybe not the actual words on the page, but I did hear them one summer, when my roommate, the Mustache, listened to the audiobook. It was over twenty-four hours long, and he would listen to it while he cooked dinner. That was the year he was obsessed with John Coltrane's album *My Favorite Things.*

He was slow to come to jazz, as was I. He was afraid it would scramble his ears, would keep him from being able to hear the blues, the music that had been his first love. Son House was his man. Skip James, too. Listening to them sing about death and poverty and love gone sideways made him happy. The blues was one of the few things that could make his smile turn up enough so that his thick mustache looked like a black caterpillar had come to rest on his lip.

My years with the Mustache were my happiest. We lived in a small apartment tucked next to a parking garage surrounded by a dense forest of oaks and cedars. I had friends outside: a fox and a possum I would share meals with under the garage, and a goldfinch that I would chirp with when I made my rounds after the Mustache returned from work in the afternoons.

He sold men's dress shoes at an outlet mall. All day long, he would measure the width and length of men's feet and keep the store tidy. He even kept a shiny metal shoehorn in his pocket, like a real pro. He had a secret passion, though. When the store was empty and all the boxes sat perfectly on their shelves, he would print a blank receipt from the register and scribble a poem on it. When he read these poems to me on our couch, I would purr in his lap, just happy that he was happy for a moment.

I'd give anything to be back on his lap, or anywhere in our home, just as long as I wasn't in this stupid box.

Where is my food?

Where is my water?

Where is my fluffy bed!

At least I have room to stand up and stretch. But really, why are the walls mirrors? Of course, it's nice to be able to see all my angles, to make sure the hairs in those impossible-to-see spots are flat and clean and all going the same way. And what's that liquid inside that glass marble with the tiniest hammer I've ever seen hanging over it? I rubbed my lips on it, because it didn't smell like anything, and everyone knows rule number one in life is that everything belongs to someone.

When I was first brought into this white room, I was shocked. It didn't smell like anything. Not human or cat, or even a spider who can live in the unseen corners behind corners.

The day I arrived at this unholy place began like any other. The Mustache was traveling to visit his mother, so the neighbor boy who would feed me when the Mustache was gone came by at first light. I watched him empty my litter box and then run the scoop lightly over the top of the clay. The Mustache had told him that if the clay wasn't perfectly flat, including in the corners, I wouldn't use the box. The result would be I would squat on the rug and leave my caca there or, worse yet, make myself sick holding it in until he returned.

The boy topped off my water bowl, taking care to make sure it was all the way to the top while also not spilling any drops on the floor. Getting my fur wet was guaranteed to ruin the rest of my day.

Next, he took my metal food bowl, which had "QUEEN" written in big purple letters on the side, and washed it. I sat and watched his hands rub away the powder and saliva from the previous day. After he dried the bowl completely, he set it down and poured a third of a scoop from my blue-and-white bag of prescription food. It was brown and shaped like pellets, nothing like the food the Mustache fed me when we first met. Those colorful bags with cartoon cats licking their chops on them contained kibble shaped like fish and stars and chickens. And even though that food didn't really taste like fish or stars or chicken, it at least tasted like something that had once been alive, like a carrot or green beans.

Since the vet had said that I had kidneys that would one day go bad, the Mustache had started to feed me these pellets that tasted like someone's idea of food. When my hunger strike hadn't worked, I relented and ate the pellets.

After I finished eating, the boy sat on the couch. He didn't turn on the TV, like he usually did, and watch *The Price Is Right.* I sat by the French doors in the sunlight and washed my face. After I had done one side, I paused, tongue sticking half out, and looked at him looking at the clock.

There wasn't anything different about the clock that would explain why he kept looking at it. It was round, the hands moved, and it ticked softly with absolute precision. The person who invented the clock clearly was descended from cats.

An hour passed, and the boy went to the garage. When he came back, he had my carrier. In the two years he had been my cat sitter, we had never gone on a trip before. He was too young to drive, so I wondered where exactly he wanted to take me.

The Mustache had bought me a black carrier made of mesh and pretend leather. He told me the mesh would let me see where we were going so that I wouldn't be scared. Sometimes the Mustache would take me on long drives in the country. Once we were in the car, he'd unzip the carrier so I could wander around and look out the windows.

The inside of his car was the color of the ash that one of his ex-girlfriends used to leave on the patio. Her cigarettes smelled worse than her breath. And that's saying something. I never knew what he saw in Miss Camel Lights. Sure, she was pretty, but nothing ever made her happy. She was even picky about socks. They were either too long or too short. Too loose or too tight. Too white or not white enough.

They met at an old record store that collected almost as much dust as it did vinyl. She had been working as a

Pity Party Planner for a few months back then. Since she had been a semiprofessionally unhappy person for years, it made sense that she'd finally put all that experience to good use and get paid for it. Ever since the cult of empathy had swept the country, people were eager to find new ways to celebrate self-sacrifice. Pity parties became all the rage. All you needed to set up shop and make money off the sadness of people was a Certificate in Emotional Statistics.

A Pity Party Planner would help you sort out all the details of your event: venue, invitations, vendors, photographer. They'd plan the menu, and, maybe most importantly, manage rude family members who tried to make themselves the center of your party because they thought they were sadder than you were.

What first caught the Mustache's eye when he turned the corner into the synth-pop aisle was a black album cover with a bunch of mouths on it. He had loved Future Islands from their earliest days. She was there to inject her Pity Party Playlist with some new music. Besides Future Islands, she also had Blind Willie Johnson, Tom Waits, Bright Eyes, Lil Wayne, and Samuel Barber, and some Major Tom David Bowie was always a hit at these sorts of parties.

After he broke the ice, he saw that she had one of his favorite 45s in her basket. The A-side had "Cotton Flower," maybe my favorite Future Islands song. The B-side had two Ed Schrader songs with thumpy bass lines. On the slipcover of the 45, there are two calicoes in an orange diamond.

I swear the cat on the bottom looks like a dude. Male calicoes are rare, which makes it even more annoying that I sometimes get mistaken for one. Just because I have wide shoulders and look like I can throw down doesn't mean I'm not a lady. One year, for my birthday, the Mustache brought this Calico 45 record home. Until the day he met Miss Camel Lights, his copy was the only one he'd ever seen in person.

She did have good taste in music. I'll give her that. When she dropped the needle one Saturday on "Please, Please, Please," I thought, "Well, well, so she knows her early James Brown. Maybe this one's a keeper."

Before my years with the Mustache, I had a whole different life. Long before I ever lived with anyone, I was sleeping under the deck behind a coffee shop when that song drifted down from a speaker attached to one of the trees. It was a live audience, probably the Apollo, and when Mr. Dynamite, The Godfather of Soul himself, growled "please," the word dripping with sweat, well, it took me back to the first time I heard a hungry tomcat. And I don't have to tell you what he was hungry for.

That tom was howling one word over and over all night long and had me trying everything I could to bust out of my house and find the Hardest-Working Cat in Show Business.

Two months later, I was tits up with a pair of kittens

drinking my milk. "My milk . . ." It took a while for me to get used to the idea that food was coming out of me. Here I was, two years old, and already with babies after my first tomcat. What a life.

The Mustache and Miss Camel Lights didn't last long. The final straw was when, one day, I wasn't moving fast enough out of her way and she nudged me with her purse. Some cheap thing that spelled Michael Kors with a "C" instead of a "K." I turned and scratched her bag. She jumped back and cried like she was hurt. I told her, "Keep it up and I'll cut you, too." All she heard was a hiss, but the fear I smelled on the back of her neck told me she knew exactly what I had said. The Mustache got between us, and I never saw her again.

Her not being around anymore to feed me when the Mustache traveled is how the neighbor boy started coming over.

When that boy unzipped the door to my carrier and sat it before me, I had no reason to go inside, so I just sat quietly.

When he put his small hands on my back and tried to nudge me in, I pretended to bite him. He jumped back. The second time he did it, I wheeled around and bit his hand. I ended our conversation with a hiss and walked away. The body can speak so much louder than words sometimes.

He ran to the kitchen, where he washed his hand and whimpered. I hoped that my teeth had gone deep enough that he would have a scar. I wanted him to never forget this moment, to remember that a second "No" comes with something extra.

I sat in a corner in what the Mustache liked to call my Great Roast Chicken position. I never took offense, because I loved it when he would read to me Carlos Drummond de Andrade's magnificent poem about Charlie Chaplin. How could any poem with roast chicken in it not be the favorite of a cat?

Most people assume the favorite poet of all cats is Christopher Smart. What cat wouldn't love these lines from "Jubilate Agno"?

> For he is of the tribe of Tiger.
> For the Cherub Cat is a term of the Angel Tiger. . . .
> For he is tenacious of his point.
> For he is a mixture of gravity and waggery.

I watched the boy dry his hands. He walked over slowly and set the carrier in front of me again. I sat up and stared at him. From his pocket, he pulled a green mouse made of felt. Inside its belly someone had poured catnip and then sewn it shut. He tossed the mouse into the back of the carrier and took a few steps back.

You can guess what happened next. I didn't want to go inside, but the body wants what the body wants. That catnip hijacked my brain, and the next thing I knew, I was as high as a kite and locked in the carrier. I pawed at the netting and tore a hole, but it was so small one of my paws wouldn't even fit through it. The last thing I remember before arriving at this lab was the boy setting me on the ground in a park and some guy in a tacky trench coat handing him an envelope.

I meowed the word "mustache."

Then the guy threw a towel over my carrier, and everything went black.

DAY 1 QUIZ

1. Do you know the names of at least two cats?
   a. Yes
   b. No
   c. Maybe

2. Do the cats talk to each other about something other than a human?
   a. Yes
   b. No
   c. Maybe

3. Have you observed one of these conversations for longer than five minutes?
   a. Yes
   b. No
   c. Maybe

4. Do you ever mention at least one of these cats in conversation without identifying their species?
   a. Yes
   b. No
   c. Maybe

5. Is one of them definitely not a magical cat?
    a. Yes
    b. No
    c. Maybe

You ever close your eyes to sleep and then can't stop thinking, so what you really crave from sleep, the not thinking, is exactly what you don't get? What a nightmare. Where is the Mustache? How is he going to find me?

I dreamed that he was kicking down the door of the trench-coat guy's house so he could beat information out of him. Who am I kidding? It's not in his nature to do something like that. Now, the woman I lived with just before him, she wasn't above cracking some skulls.

She was a sculptor from Baltimore. Part of why we bonded is because we both felt Michelangelo was a hack painter. Maybe I would feel differently if I saw the Sistine Chapel in person. I doubt it, though. I just don't understand how people let him get away with those frescoes. The man never painted a torso that wasn't as wide as a camel-back trunk.

Even if you look at the most famous of the frescoes, the best part is the detail of Adam's and God's hands. But if you zoom out and look at their torsos, forget about it. Both Adam and God have hips that are the same width as their shoulders. And don't get me started on how God's left arm is way longer than the right, or how Adam's foot looks like a cow hoof.

I know what the apologists say: that it's all the fault of the surface, that painting upside down on a rounded surface would make it difficult for anyone to nail the proportions of the human body. And then there's the camp that says bodies were different back then, and you can't judge by today's standards, blah-blah-blah.

Way I see it, you're either a master painter or you're not.

I mean, if you're on the fence about whether or not Michelangelo was a two-bit hack who couldn't paint a normal-looking human body, just look at his sculptures.

His *David* is sublime.

The valley of his chest is glorious. The shoulders are strong but subtle, not unlike a thunderhead in the distance. David's curly hair is majestic and perfectly frames his face, which says, "You talkin' to me?"

The body of David is a living, breathing rock. The *Pietà* is the same, only he took the degree of difficulty up a notch by carving out of marble cloth so real that you half expect the wind would rustle it if you opened the door.

Vermeer is my man. It doesn't get much better in painting than his milkmaid. I can hear that thick milk dribbling from the pitcher. What I wouldn't give for a saucer of milk right now. Or a drop of water.

The Sculptor from Baltimore used a water cooler in

one exhibit. While she was trying to find just the right one, the loft we shared was filled with water coolers. I made a game of trying to get water out of the spigots.

The day she found out she had scored exhibit space at the Museum of Natural History's twenty-first-century wing, we celebrated. Crab cakes and slaw for her, and fresh fish for me. I really believed in her work, even if I didn't always understand it.

When the first week of the exhibit was a wrap, she came home and played a recording. The space had been designed to look like any typical office space, only all the furniture was missing. But you could just imagine the cubicles and the workers who would rather have been anywhere else but there. In the center of the room sat a water cooler.

Although you couldn't see any faces, only the backs of people, voices from the audience drifted in.

"It's a metaphor for the modern personality," said a man.

"No, it's the perfect marriage of form and content," said a woman in a beret.

While people rubbed their chins and tried to look smart, the Sculptor, who had been hiding among the crowd, crossed the velvet rope. She untied her shoes and kicked them into the crowd. Then she pulled off her Springsteen T-shirt. She still lived as a man back then, so it wasn't a big deal. Finally, she wriggled out of her pants. I can only imagine what the audience thought as they looked at her standing there in what looked like a puffy diaper made out of wool.

She then knelt with her mouth under the spigot, and drank and drank and drank. And, just like that, she made two and a half gallons disappear.

She'd learned through trial and error that emptying a five-gallon cooler into her body at one stretch could be fatal. When the ambulance drove her off the night she learned what water intoxication was, I thought, "How foolish can one human be?" The simple things humans have to learn the hard way never cease to amaze me.

At the museum, she waddled around the room and pointed at her giant belly. The orange lights softened, and then the second part of her exhibit began as she started studying the faces of the people in the crowd, turning over in her mind their expressions.

When we got to this part of the recording, she pulled me onto her lap, rubbed my ears, and said, "This is when the fun begins and the audience becomes the real exhibit."

I perked up when I saw a man with eyebrows that looked like cockroaches. He was wearing a Members Only jacket. Lord knows what museum he stole that from. He walked up to the Sculptor and said, "This is bullshit."

The Sculptor's head bobbed side to side like my tail does when I'm trying to mesmerize a bird. It was obvious Cockroach Eyebrows didn't know what to say or do. Then he poked her belly with his finger. She squatted down and started sniffing his finger. Then she bit it! He yanked his hand back and yelled. And the Sculptor—she just grinned.

She was nuts, and I really loved her crazy ass.

Security guards dressed in blue rushed to the guy and carried him away. After that, the rest of the people wandered off until there was no one left. She bowed, in her always very theatrical way, and then bolted for the bathroom.

I didn't get how this was art, but it made her happy. And that's all that mattered to me.

Happiness wasn't a regular thing around our house. There was the needy squirrel in the backyard that always made her smile. That thing would climb up the crooked telephone pole, shimmy over on a wire, and squeak until the Sculptor came to the window and dropped some peanuts on the ground for it.

The Sculptor got a kick out of watching that squirrel chew through a peanut like a buzz saw, bits of shell flying out both sides of its mouth. She even gave the squirrel a name: Manos. She called it this because that fool thing would stand up on its hind legs and reach its hands up toward our upstairs window as if it could grab the peanuts.

I admit it was all a little funny. What would've been

funnier is if the Sculptor had let me loose down there. We would've found out real quick if that gourmet diet of peanuts had slowed down that squeaker or not.

Most times when we sat down to watch TV, it was to watch Dirty Harry movies. I don't know what she liked about them. Okay, watching them once is one thing, but week after week? It was almost like the darker the scenes, the better she felt? I know because her pulse would slow down and her breath would go from her normal jitteriness to even and light. Usually, by the time the really dark scenes started, I was asleep in her lap, dreaming.

Sure, it was nice to see the bad guys get what was coming to them, but my favorite part of those movies was the music. Lalo Schifrin was one cool cat from Argentina. He could make the dark scenes darker, but he could also make music so light and with so much jump that I could practically see the notes bebopping in the air.

Lemme guess: you're placing your bets that my favorite Eastwood movies were the monkey ones, right? Wrong. What makes you think that a cat would like a goofy ape? Sure, it was cute how they had him tear those cars apart with his hands. I bet some people even watched that monkey scrapping a Caddy and thought that was real. Humans will believe just about anything.

My favorite movie was *The Gauntlet.* Unlike in Dirty Harry, Eastwood plays a cop who's a real bum, a cop whose body count in the movie is a perfect goose egg. He's a drunk who can't do anything right and who should've just quit. It's a chase movie, which is pretty much every cat's favorite movie genre. His character, Ben, has to drive a witness from Vegas to Phoenix. Some bad dudes don't want them to make it. Simple, no?

Sondra Locke plays the witness. Her name is Gus Mally, and she's sharp and spunky and beautiful. While working as a prostitute, she overhears some stuff from clients in the Mob that she wasn't supposed to hear, I guess. I dunno, it's been a long time since I've seen it.

The part that's always stuck with me, though, is when this wretched cop asks Gus what it's like being a hooker. The creep is just asking for it, and she delivers. She tells him she always thought it was a lot like being a cop, says the only difference is she can take a long bath and come out clean as the day she was born. But a flunky cop like him has rot in his brain, and no amount of water on earth can clean it off. And then she twists the knife perfectly and says, "I know you don't like women like me. We're a bit aggressive. We frighten you. But that's only because you got filth in your brain and I'm afraid the only way you'll ever clean it out is to put a bullet through it."

That cop yowls like he's been stabbed and almost crashes the car they're in. I could watch that beautiful creature Sondra Locke all day long. If reincarnation is real, then Locke was either a cat before she was born a human, or a cat body was waiting for her on the other side of her life.

At the end of the movie, they ride into Phoenix on a

bus they stole. But not before cops fill it with thousands of bullets. Humans and their guns. They figured that bus was gonna be their coffin, but they were wrong, and the good guys won the day again.

What the hell is this box I'm in??? What kind of a psychopath builds a box with mirrors for all the inner walls? That trench-coat guy better not have kidnapped me for some demented art project. I'm tired of scratching the glass and getting nowhere. I can't tip the box—it's anchored somehow. And I can't cut the walls open. I've meowed so much my throat feels like it's shrunk and also like it's on fire.

Maybe this is what humans call feeling hoarse. I just always assumed the expression meant the person felt like a giant beast with long, beautiful legs and a bad attitude.

I know there are people nearby because I sense them. It's not that I can smell or hear them, exactly. Humans give off an energy that can never be mistaken for another animal's. It's not an aura, either. It's more like a hum that you can feel, like when you catch your tail in a door and, in addition to being swollen and hurting like hell, it also pulses. But you can't see it pulsing, only feel it.

It's the same with humans. I can feel the hum of a human a block away. And what I'm sensing now is five hums, either sitting or standing, in a semicircle around whatever this contraption is that I'm stuck in.

I wonder if they can hear me. If only they could, I might have a chance at convincing one of them to let me out. A long time ago, the first cat to wander into the cave of a human and make itself at home learned how to meow in the same frequency as human babies. Not surprisingly, since that first cat chirped, humans haven't been able to resist stroking our fur and sharing their food with us and letting us snuggle in their beds. Knowing how to hijack the nurturing instinct of humans is not genetic, though. It's a skill taught from one cat to another.

What if the people outside the box can hear my meows and are still doing nothing to free me? That would make them less than human if it was true. Or maybe their instincts have gone haywire. Or—and this is a frightening thought—they are some kind of new human with different instincts, the kind of human who could ignore the chatter of a baby. That's the kind of creature I'd prefer never to cross paths with, thank you very much.

I miss the beforelife. The Mustache introduced me to that expression. He was always taking expressions and flipping them on their heads. The "afterlife" becomes the "beforelife." "Burn it all down" becomes "water it all down." And so on.

One day, the Mustache came home from work with a new book called *The Beforelife.* It had an ugly sticker on the cover with $3.99 on it. He'd never read to me any poems by Franz Wright before. He'd picked the book up at a store that sold the books other stores had not been able to sell.

I'll never forget that night. The air was sharp because

it had rained during dinner. He had cooked something special because it was my fourteenth birthday. Beef enchiladas with red sauce for him, and this exquisite smoked goat cheese from Spain with a side of refried beans and rice. For me, he served up a pâté of Nova Scotian duck made by some company up north. Liver, heart, bone broth—it had all the tastiest bits.

Only thing better would've been catching one of these ducks myself. In my youth, I could've done it. Back then, I could jump high enough to snatch a foolish bird out of the air, one who'd miscalculated how much time it needed to fly away. There's nothing that reminds you of your place in the world like catching your own food, separating feather and fur from the muscle, the muscle from the bone, and finally the bone from the spirit.

The Mustache never really knew when I was born. Heck, I didn't even know that, but he picked a day and year and we went with that and I loved him all the more for it.

"Apples have wings, true or false," is the one line that has stuck with me all these years from *The Beforelife,* because it is maybe the most cat thing a human has ever written. Maybe ole Franz had some Maine coon in his family tree.

The next morning, the Mustache was saying "Apples have wings" over and over as he dressed for work. It was almost like a prayer.

This went on for a week, and then one day he returned

from work with another copy of Wright's book. I sniffed it to be sure. I thought maybe he was going to give it as a gift. I watched him, my tail swishing, as he carefully removed the sticker and then wiped the cover gently with some smelly orange liquid. Somehow, he made this new book look even newer. That weekend, he drove to Castle Books and pretended he had bought the book there, but didn't like it, and wanted to exchange it for something else. He did this seven times over the next year, coming home with Nazim Hikmet and a yellow Sharon Olds book with shells on the cover that I liked to nudge off the kitchen table.

I was proud of him in a way, for how he thought everything out like a hunter. He would only try this swap just after the store had opened because he reasoned that the clerks would assume all dishonest people were still asleep. My Mustache would've never tried this at the other stores, but the fact that Castle required their employees to dress up as minor literary characters made him feel that maybe, just maybe, they wouldn't have minded his little deception if he got caught. He would've made a fine cat, except for his regret. He never could let that go.

Before you judge my sweet Mustache too harshly, I offer as a defense that he didn't have much money. Surely much less than other humans I had lived with. What's more, he reasoned that Castle would be able to sell ole Franz's books easily, because they were basically still new and the poems were incredible. His dream was that one day he'd become a poet, too, and have a book and read at Castle to his fans. And if he was really successful, so many of his books would flood the market that they, too, would end up at the sad castaway bookstores. Then, in a twist of fate worthy of a Borges story, a young aspiring writer would buy his book on the cheap and also swap it at Castle for the latest poetry stars. "Now, that would be real success," the Mustache would say.

But then Castle closed all their locations nationwide. The store going out of business meant he lost all hope of his dream ever coming true. He stopped writing, and took his mother's advice to find a real career. He got his certification in something called Emotional Statistics and was quickly hired as an Emotional Support Human.

The country was at war back then, so there was plenty of work for Emotional Support Humans. His first gig was at the airport. He'd show up at 7:00 a.m., slip on his yellow vest and a collar with tags. The tags had his name, height, and weight. Before he left the house, he would have already painted his face to look like a bear's. Emotional Support Humans who worked for the airlines could choose whatever animal they wanted. He chose a bear because he thought it would make people remember the stuffed animals they'd had as children.

People who were nervous about flying would wade through Security and at their gate request an Emotional Support Human. Once the passenger had paid the extra charge and was cleared to fly with an ESH, the ESH would walk over on all fours. The passenger then attached their leash to complete the arrangement, and the human flew with the passenger to their destination. If the passenger wasn't a high roller and couldn't spring for an extra seat for you, then you had to be a really small human so you could sit on someone's lap comfortably or worse be stuffed under the seat in front of them. Since having something to pet was the whole point of calming down a nervous flyer, if you were under the seat, then the human often slipped one shoe off and petted you with their foot in order to relax. The Mustache had history books that described how animals, mostly dogs, had been the first emotional-support companions before bans outlawing the practice had been passed. I'm glad I wasn't around for that.

This job took the Mustache all over, and he got to meet all sorts of interesting people. You'd be amazed at who gets nervous flying and who doesn't. It's not the old maid from some Podunk town who's never flown before. Nope, it's the CEO of a multinational conglomerate who has tens of thousands of people working for them. Go figure.

The Mustache didn't last even two months before he was fired. For starters, he wasn't small enough to fit under the seat, so he was expensive. But what really did him in was that he kept violating the cardinal rule of the job: don't speak unless you're spoken to. And even when he followed the rule, he was so hungry to talk to someone, anyone, that he'd talk really fast and forget what he was saying; then, in order to jog his memory, he'd say "Rewind!" and do all of the movements from the last minute backward. He'd even pronounce the words that he did remember backward. Needless to say, a human who is more nervous than you and who is constantly putting themselves on rewind is the last person that a nervous passenger wants around. And can you blame them?

Do I have to say that the Mustache was a depressive? Had been all his life, I suspect. Troubled childhood, that sort of thing. He never really learned how to receive love. He would do and do for the women he loved, but never let them do for him.

He would've been a complete sad sack if not for the fact that he was handsome. Not in any kind of obvious way, mind you. He didn't have the perfectly symmetrical face of actors, and wasn't buff from spending hours upon hours in the gym. No, he was handsome in the old ways. There was an elegance to the way his body moved. Even his thinking face had its charms. His other saving grace was that he accepted—no, cherished—my love for him.

Cat love is so imperfect, and yet it's almost perfect because of this. Cat love is like a rainbow in the sense that even though you can't see the half of the rainbow that is hidden underground, you feel grateful for what your senses do allow you to take into your body.

To experience the totality of a rainbow would be madness for a human. The body would be so overcome that the mind would forget itself, forget the rainbow, so that when one was broken from this trance, one would have only the vaguest memory of color and warmth.

Cat love is like this.

DAY 2 QUIZ

1. "Love is a _______ old heart disease." (Son House)
   a. sweet
   b. sleepy
   c. worried

2. "I'm _______ and full of love." (Roethke)
   a. odd
   b. green
   c. flying

3. "Love is or it ain't. ______ love ain't love at all." (Morrison)
   a. Hungry
   b. Thin
   c. Blind

4. "Love is _______ on fire." (Sontag)
   a. friendship
   b. reason
   c. bodies

5. "Love is sharing your ______." (Schultz)
   a. pillow
   b. clothes
   c. popcorn

The room is empty. The hum of the lightbulbs is gone. The hum of the sun, too. I don't know how long I've been sleeping.

I'm so thirsty.

I want to go home.

I miss the Mustache. Miss the corduroy bed he bought for my birthday with the lining that feels like a sheep.

Miss the back of the closet in the room with all his books. Under his hanging pants, in the corner, is one of my favorite places in the world. When he almost closes the door and the lights are off and the house is empty, I can barely hear or see anything.

It's pure bliss.

The Mustache calls it my fortress of solitude. I like the Man Without Fear more than Superman so I like to think of it as my Daredevil deprivation chamber.

I've always found Superman just so stiff. If you look at the world through his eyes, everything that's good and bad fits neatly in labeled boxes. But the world doesn't work that way. Life taught me that lesson early on. And if

I ever forget it, life is waiting around every corner to teach it to me again until it sticks.

When I lived under the deck of the coffee shop with my two babies, you'd be surprised how people treated us. I always made my babies stay back, even if someone seemed nice.

Some people would give us bits of meat from the sandwiches they didn't finish. They'd rip off a piece and say, "Here, kitty, kitty." When I just sniffed the air and stared at them from under the deck, they'd try to coax me again. When they finally gave up, they'd toss the meat near me.

Even though the meat was now covered in dirt, I ate it. And the people who did the tossing, they'd say "Awwww" and "How cute" and stupid stuff like that as they watched me eat dirty food that they could have placed on some grass instead.

This is what passes for kindness in humans.

It can always be worse, though. One night, some kids were jumping around and laughing on the deck long after the coffee shop had closed. They would've sounded like giant horses to my babies if they had known what horses were. Next thing we knew, the kids were dropping their pants and pissing in the water bowl the owners of the coffee shop had put out for us. I never thought those boys and girls would stop giggling and leave.

If I knew where they were now, I'd teach them a little something about tenderness.

Not all humans we saw were like this. Lucky Charms

was nice. She came every Friday to fill our water bowl and give us kibble. Every now and then, she'd even bring a can of wet food for us.

We saw her so often that I even let my babies go near her. She was the first human I ever touched. I still remember the day like it was yesterday.

It was the first morning that had felt chilly since winter. My babies and I were curled up tight when we heard her voice. Usually, we were ready to greet her when we heard the rumble of her car, but that morning she snuck up on us.

She was wearing baggy sweatpants and a Guns N' Roses tank top. Later, she introduced me to their music. "November Rain" was the one song she could play all day and never get tired of.

Her hair was up in a bun and her bangs swooped across her forehead like a waterfall. She wore green sandals and smelled like nachos.

As she walked toward the deck, she made her usual clicking sounds with her tongue to announce herself to us. I heard her first and jumped up while my babies curled tighter and licked their tiny lips.

After she filled our water and food bowls, Lucky Charms got on one knee and called me over. I was within a foot of her, and I wanted to touch her more than anything, but I was afraid. Not afraid that she would hurt me, but afraid of what it would mean. Of who I would become.

She extended her arm and reached out a single finger. The tip of her finger was the same size as my nose. I sniffed it but didn't touch it. Then she lifted her arm up and rubbed her fingers together and clicked her tongue again. I stood on my hind legs, reached up, and rubbed my cheek on her fingers.

When she ran her warm hand over my head and down my back and then up my tail with a swoosh, everything changed.

I was in heaven.

There's a very clear line in the cat world when it comes to humans. In one moment, I had crossed from one side of the line to the other. And I had taken my babies with me across that line. There was no going back.

One day, people stopped showing up to the coffee shop. No customers and no workers. As much as I loved the music from their speakers in the trees, the peace and quiet was nice.

Soon the only human we saw was Lucky Charms. When she told us that the coffee shop had gone out of business and that the land and building had been sold to a developer who was going to knock everything down and build some apartments, I didn't have a clue what any of that meant. I was still new to learning about how humans will so easily throw things and people aside when they have no more use for them. It was like someone had decided that our home, and everything in it, including us and the trees and the building, were trash.

My babies were off milk and were growing fast. One had already wandered off to a house a couple blocks down the road and had a good thing going. He was a handsome silver tom with a long tail. They let him sleep under the porch and gave him food for keeping the mice away. My other baby always stayed near his momma. He was my fluffy black shadow.

When the day came for us to go with Lucky Charms, she didn't even need to use the long metal trap in the back seat of her car. She opened up a carrier, and we walked right in, and she took us home.

Living with her was a trip. Not because her house was weird or because she was any different at home than she was when we'd see her at the coffee shop, but because we'd never been inside a human building before.

Her house was old. I could sense at least ten generations of cats around it.

The windows were tall. And so was the ceiling. Her house was really just one big room, because it had been a school a long time ago. On still days, when I was the only one in the house and nothing was moving, not even the wind down the hill through the faraway trees, I would sit in the window, in my Great Roast Chicken position, and the building would tell me its secrets.

All of a sudden, the room is full of children sitting at their desks. Two sweethearts in the back whisper to each other. Others focus on the lesson and write their names in shaky letters over and over.

This wasn't my memory, or even the memory of any human still living, but it was a memory nonetheless. Mountains and the grass and animals aren't the only things that remember. The sky remembers. Wood remembers. Glass remembers. The nails that hold them all together remember.

The memory always ends with the same people saying the same things. A little boy with curly hair raises his hand. The teacher says, "Yes, Johnathan?"

"My neck hurts, Miss. I'm tired of writing."

"You don't write with your neck, Johnathan."

The kids giggle. The teacher hushes them and says, "You can lay your head on your desk, Johnathan."

And he does.

And the room is empty again for now.

Our first weeks with Lucky Charms were bliss. She'd wake up and work from home all morning. Then, after she had for lunch her second bowl of cereal for the day, we'd go outside and play. Then came a nap and then dinner. My baby who wasn't a baby anymore would sleep with me in a little cat yurt Lucky Charms made for us. She covered us up before turning out the lights and climbing the ladder up to her loft, where she slept like a bird high above us in a cozy nest.

We didn't have many visitors in those early days. Then, one week, Lucky Charms stopped working. Another week passed, and still no work. And then her momma came to visit.

"Hey, sweetie, are you sure about this?"

"Yeah, Momma. I can't take care of both of them anymore."

"But won't she be lonely when you're gone during the day if I take her baby to live with me?"

"I don't know. They sleep a lot. And you can always bring him over on the weekends so they can see each other."

"Okay."

"I just know with this new job I might be gone a lot. I'm running out of money, and I need to try something."

"I know."

"At least this job will keep me out of the draft."

"Gracias a Dios."

"Last thing I want to do is go fight a war that don't make no sense."

"I'll pray for you, *mija*."

"Thanks, Momma."

"Okay, where is this *cabrón*?"

And then, just like that, my fluffy black shadow was gone. I wasn't sad, and he wasn't, either. He was a he and I was his momma, and even though Lucky Charms's house was airy, we needed space. He needed room to grow into the graceful tom he was already becoming. Lucky Charms's momma lived alone, so he had that whole house to himself.

The day after my baby left, Lucky Charms started her new job as an Emotional Support Human. The unemployment office had sent her home with a box of newspapers, flour, salt, paint, and some brushes.

I played with some feathers she hung from the back of an old chair while she cut newspapers into long strips. I love the sound of scissors cutting through paper, especially when it's thin, like newspaper. I found the news itself boring, because all the stories were the same. Each one had the same picture of seven women holding guns and dressed in green-brown uniforms that resembled some human's idea of what a pile of leaves in autumn would look like. Only women could own guns or serve in the military, and my Lucky Charms had no interest in guns. Or in dressing like a compost pile in autumn.

When she finished cutting all the papers and walked to the kitchen to start mixing flour and water into a paste, the blue-and-white vertical stripes of her jumper straightened out, and, what can I say, this made me glad. So glad, in fact, that I started purring at the sight of those stripes, which reminded me of a long wall of window blinds and the vast ocean on the other side. No, this new job had to work out so she could keep from being drafted.

The next morning, she slipped my leash on and put me in her car, along with a bag of paints and brushes. Buckled into the passenger seat was something made out of the newspapers and the glue that had the same shape as Lucky Charms. Only it had no legs. It had nothing from the waist down.

It also didn't have a face.

Or hair.

Or the smell a living, breathing body carries until the day it stops living and breathing.

I refused to let it touch me, because it was strange and I didn't want my scent attached to it.

On the other side of town, we rode an elevator and walked around until we found a door with a bunch of flower circles laid beside it. Lucky Charms knocked a few times, and we were let in.

The smell of grief on the man and woman who lived there was overwhelming. It was so strong that I started sneezing. They had never seen a cat sneeze before, I guess, judging by the way they looked at me. Lucky Charms walked over to their kitchen table and said, "Which chair is your daughter's?" They pointed at the chair nearest the window. Lucky Charms set her paper-and-glue torso in the chair. The couple gave her a picture of their daughter that was taken the day she graduated from basic training. Lucky Charms pulled out her paints and rummaged through her bag until she found one the same color as their daughter's skin. She then said, "Do you have the hair?"

They brought out a bag of their daughter's hair. I didn't like the way they looked at Lucky Charms, as if they wanted to ask a question they knew better than to ask, something like, "Why are you here while our daughter is over there, lost, without us, without even a decent burial?"

By the time Lucky Charms's brush touched the paper person for the first time, I was asleep. I'd had some catnip before we left, and I couldn't keep my eyes open. Before long, I couldn't hear the neighbor blasting Taylor Swift upstairs or the swallows trapped in the floor. Even the Vivaldi their parakeet was whistling went from a background sound to barely there to just gone.

In my dreams, I saw a world without any colors except for green. Green skin. Green clouds. Green water. A green sun. In this world, the only time people called the police was when a cat forgot how to climb down from a tree. No more cops choking people on the street. No more jails and prisons. No more wars. No more funerals with empty boxes.

When Lucky Charms woke me up, I was about to lick green ice cream from a green spoon left on a green picnic table.

The paper person now had long black hair and a face. Her mouth reminded me of a crooked sunflower. She was wearing a faded white T-shirt that said "Texas Babe" on it.

Before we got in the car, Lucky Charms picked me up and pointed to the window, where Paper Girl sat at the kitchen table, waiting for her parents to serve her a plate of food. A plate of food she would never eat.

That was the last time I went with Lucky Charms to work. I couldn't take those homes dripping with grief anymore. It's just too much, especially when the humans are doing so little to pull themselves out of it. If they were cats, they'd be sad but still out climbing trees and licking themselves. I bet some of the people in those houses Lucky Charms visits haven't washed in weeks. No thanks, I'd rather be at home asleep in my sunlight with my tall ceilings and dreaming I have wings.

This box will be the death of me. I can feel the five hums surrounding the box. Surrounding me.

It feels like years since I ate or drank anything. How did I get here?

Where are my babies?

I need my babies.

Us hear the bird so high above the deck talk tree.
Another bird talk tree back.
Us smile.

Us move milk.
Us lick us from baby pink bodies us hungry hungry for us.

Another bird talk tree.

Us dark.
Us tongue us.
Us work warm belly.

Another bird talk.

. . .

Push.
Push.
Push.

Another bird.

Us love purr milk purr.
Us love purr milk.
Us love purr.
Us love.

Another.

Us.

Another

Us

Us

Us

DAY 3 QUIZ

1. When I dream I am flying to paradise, a cat waits at home for me.
   a. True
   b. False
   c. Maybe

2. A flock of seagulls is sadder than Goya, who is sadder than Björk, who is sadder than a cherry tree in spring.
   a. True
   b. False
   c. Maybe

3. When a history book mentions a mass shooting, I feel lucky.
   a. True
   b. False
   c. Maybe

4. When I wear mascara, my suffering is greater than that of a donkey painted to look like a zebra.
   a. True
   b. False
   c. Maybe

5. The fear I have of not boiling an egg long enough is related to my fear of death.
   a. True
   b. False
   c. Maybe

What is another cat doing in this box? And how the hell did they get it in here without waking me up?

Hiss.

Nothing.

What is that squeak? A pencil? There it is again. Two squeaks now.

Jeezuz, is this cat dead? Is this some kind of a sick joke? Should I touch it? What if it's made out of paper and glue? Did some sicko make a cat dummy that's supposed to look like me? Is that what the five hums outside the box have been doing this whole time while I've been locked up in here, starving to death? More like five bums.

Should I stand on three legs, one paw up, ready to plant down so I can jump up (this is a technique some mammals, such as myself, use to startle predators or opponents, whatever the case may be, who are either larger than us, or frightening, or both), or extend slowly and tap this cat thing in the box with me?

All right, I'm gonna do it. I hold this position for what feels like hours and then: tap.

It doesn't move.

Tap.

It's not paper and glue. But it is stiff and cold.

I sniff my toes that touched the cat thing when I tapped it on its back. It does have real fur. This fur carries a perfume made of equal parts fear and exhaustion and hunger and urine. There is also the scent of the Mustache. And our home and my couch and my bowl, and the moon when it peeks in through the skylight. And a trace of my babies. And my momma and daddy, and all of it is me somehow.

So there she is, a tortoiseshell cat, betrayed by the neighbor boy, kidnapped by a man in a trench coat, sleeping in a box as if she didn't have a care in the world, as if she'd just splayed on a sidewalk in autumn right over a line of ants and started licking them up one by one as if they were the most delicious thing in the world a cat could eat. Not a catch of stinky shrimp on the deck of a boat, or a young mockingbird that still hadn't learned how to respect the laws of gravity and claws. And what does a cat that could be confused for a hell mouth in the vast chronicles of the Kingdom of Ants do after dispatching so many unsuspecting souls? Well, the cat curls like a nautilus, like the one in this box, and sleeps.

If she's me, then who am I? Are she and I now some we?

I want to cuddle her, because she will never see the Mustache again, will never sit in his soft lap while he strokes her head and she relishes the cold and lovely feel of his blue mesh shorts against her pink stomach, and of his hand—that soft, giant hand—stroking her head in the firm and loving way her momma's rough pink tongue used to. Poor thing, we won't ever know any of this again.

I cuddle next to her, tucking into the circle of her nautilus, and I stretch my arms to try and hold her, to pull her tight, closer, as close as possible, but my arms are too short, and so I keep on reaching until they stretch like chewing gum that won't let the bottom of a shoe go. They wrap around her neck, and under, and look, now they are the color of limes, not the deep green of ripe limes, but the yellow-green of young limes, limes that still haven't forgotten that the tart energy that flows inside their rinds once fell from the sky, and cold outer space before that, and the center of the roiling sun before even that.

My legs are long enough that I can now hold her so tight and close that I am almost hugging the both of us, and look, my toes are orange now. I hug us so tight that I feel my back crack. It cracks again. Again and again. I should cry, but it doesn't hurt. My back is growing out, and round, growing over my hips and shoulders, until I see a shell like a rising sun peek over my shoulder.

The mirrors inside the box tell the whole story. I have a shell on my back made of three bands. It's blue, but not the kind of blue you would think. It's like the blue of a swimming pool at night that's lit by lamps in the water so that the color is aqua, but light aqua, an aqua pulled so far past the edge of itself that it's almost a white-blue, a color that has forgotten itself and where it comes from and where it could go.

I hold her like this with this new body tighter than I have ever held anyone for what feels like forever. Tighter than I ever held my babies. Even tighter than I ever held my momma. As I open my eyes and stretch my new legs out as far as I can, I see my feet go past the wall of my box and disappear. I quickly pull them back and lick my orange toes. They used to be black and pink, but now they're as bright as the pulp of a clementine.

They taste fine. But how did I do that? And where did my feet go?

The last of the hums has stopped. I've been flicking the tip of my tail in and out of the box. My tail up is in the box and, when down, through the wall and out of the box. I've been doing this for hours, to see if they'd notice. I did it fast and slow, waited thirty seconds between flicks, then sixty, then flicked thirty, sixty, thirty. Still nada, zilch.

Unless they're brain-dead out there, I would think that the tip of a green cat tail popping in and out of the box they've been staring at for four days would get someone's attention.

I can't believe this is how it all ends. In a fucking box. And not even a box on the side of the road, where I was tossed because my vet bills were too expensive, or because I clawed up all the fancy Pier 1 furniture, and someone thought the best thing for all parties concerned was to take me "on a drive to the country." You know the old song and dance. "She'll be fine! It's a return to nature! She'll find a nice barn and have more mice to hunt and eat than in her wildest dreams!"

You wanna know what my wildest dreams were like? For starters, they contained no boxes. Not a single one. Least of all a box with mirrors for the inside walls. That's the stuff of nightmares.

My dreams have, or had, I guess, who knows if I can even still dream now? Or sleep, for that matter! Do I have to sleep? Can I sleep if I feel like it even if this new body doesn't need it? I guess I'll find out the answer to that question eventually.

But dreams—yes, dreams—my dreams had grass, open skies, a breeze, and blue butterflies. And my best dream? My best dream had all these things, plus a tree. But not just any tree, a cedar taller than any tree I have ever climbed, a cedar of Lebanon.

Taller than any building I've ever lived in; its branches at its waist are longer than a school bus, tip to tip. When the cedar of Lebanon appears in my dreams, I climb it, and something happens that never happens when I'm awake. The birds keep singing. Not songs of alarm or woe, but songs of love and joy. And the birds are hoopoes, birds that I have never seen in person, only in pictures, so I don't know if the song those silly-looking pink birds sing in my dreams is really their song or not. It doesn't matter, because what is most important is the singing as

I shimmy up the trunk and then walk out along a branch where I will stretch out and scratch my chin on the mossy bark. As much as I have always loved the taste of fresh bird—I've known some odd cats who never had the stomach for it—I like the sound of birdsong just as much, if not more, even.

A human hasn't been born yet who can rival the beauty that spills from the throat of a tanager or a mockingbird. Or a starling, that bag of jewels with wings that warms a sad winter day with its song. Queen Aretha comes close. Pavarotti, too. But close only counts in horseshoes and hand grenades. The tip of my tail is about the size of a grenade now. And just as green.

I want to see what's on the other side of this box, but I don't want to leave her, me, in this box by herself. I waited for so long for someone to find me and free me, and the last person I ever expected to come find me in here was, well, me. My mind is racing with questions. If I leave the box

. . . can I return?

. . . will I forget who I am?

. . . am I still a cat?

. . . will I be able to touch my body?

. . . am I a body anymore?

. . . will I forget the wind?

. . . will I forget the grass?

. . . will I forget the Mustache?

. . . am I a body anymore?

. . . am I still a cat?

. . . can I return?

. . . can I?

. . . can?

. . . can someone please tell me who made the decision that, on this day, in this year, of this century, I would go to sleep in a lab, not wake up, and never return to my home or my beloved Mustache or to the quiet life of love and joy and silence that I had so gratefully settled into? Who made that decision for me, and where are they, so that I can play with them like a mouse from here until kingdom come. If anyone ever deserved it, it's that human.

What's waiting for me outside this box? What if it's the human heaven, a place where animals and trees are just ornaments to remind them of what they've left behind. Cats don't believe in heaven, because we don't need to. Human heaven is for suckers who look around at this gorgeous world we live in and think, "There's gotta be something better than this." You think a cheetah slashes across the savanna like a bolt of spotted lightning and thinks, "There's gotta be something better than this?" You think a tiger that takes a dip in a cool spring after climbing a tree to swat at a helicopter is thinking, "I can't wait to die so that I can really start living"? Not a chance. The cheetah and tiger are living their best lives.

You never hear cats going on and on about some massive hall filled with cat warriors drinking mead, or a paradise of pillows full of cat virgins. Humans have been around long enough that this shouldn't be news, but some of them are real sickies. For some, paradise is where the lion will lay down next to a lamb and there will be no bloodshed. Such fools. Don't they know that there are cats and lambs that do that now, as in today, here, on this good green earth?

If you ask me, paradise is here.

I wonder if there are other cats in boxes out there right now. This box is my coffin; well, it's the coffin for my body, at least. I don't want to leave her.

"I won't be gone long. I promise." Time to have a look around. Here goes nothin'.

Now the tip of my nose.

Now one paw.

I close my eyes and carry me and this big blue shell on my back into the unknown.

The penguin and the polar bear are mocking me from the AN EYE FOR AN EYE MAKES THE WORLD GO BLIND poster on the wall.

I feel like I've seen that bird somewhere else. He's no regular penguin. He's one of those Hollywood animals with an agent and a hairdresser and riders that include buckets of sardines in his trailer. I bet you he and that bear are probably repped by the same agency.

Get those two actors hungry enough and one of them will be chomping on eyes and everything else in no time flat. It's the way of the world. Animals can pretend to live like humans as much as they want, pretend that they've forgotten what it feels like to study the wind for the faintest scent or sound of the thing you most want to eat or that most wants to eat you. You can't pretend away those kinds of instincts, no matter how hard you try. And that's a good thing, because humans can be just as vicious as any bear or penguin.

What, you think a penguin can't be vicious because you put them in cartoons and have them tap-dancing like Sammy Davis, Jr.? Just ask krill or a squid what it feels like to have your body sliced and yanked apart by a mouth like scissors while you're still alive.

That's it! That penguin does commercials for some new brand of fabric softener. What a sellout.

When I land on the floor, I immediately lose my balance and roll forward into the wall. Not only will I have to get used to the weight of this blue condo on my back, but to these long green legs, too. The table the box is on isn't very high, and still the ground came at me a lot faster than I'm used to.

Under the table, I can see five pairs of feet. The long tubes of light in the ceiling make everything brighter than it should be. I tiptoe under the table and peek out at the humans in their chairs. When I sneeze, I realize that there was no need to tiptoe, because either they're deaf as doornails or they can't see me.

I meow, and it sounds like no meow that's ever come out of my mouth. I try again, and I'm reminded of an egg bubbling in a skillet. A few more times, and my meow is mostly back. My babies wouldn't recognize it, but no matter, because smell is what counts. Wait, do I still have a scent? Surely, death never stopped anything from smelling. If anything, it amplifies, but who knows how any of this works. Where's my Virgil, my guide through all this insanity?

I walk over to the closest human and sniff his black shoes. The soles are thick, and I can practically smell the arthritis in his hips. But there's something else, too. Nectarine? No, it's faint, but it's Mexican yellow cake with the pink icing. I'd know that smell anywhere.

A bell rings, and suddenly the five hums get up from their chairs. I jump out of the way as they collect their backpacks and start for the door. I take one last look at the box on the table with me inside it, and follow Mr. Pink out the door.

From the back seat of his car, he adjusts the bottle of FEEL WTR in the console over and over. It's almost like he's trying to place it just so, so that the donkey grinning on the label is staring at him.

He relocks the doors, adjusts the mirrors, shifts and reshifts in his seat, and then we're off.

A voice on the radio says, "If you feel like you have a deficiency of feeling, then east of the Mississippi dial 1-800-FEELING and west of the Mississippi dial 1-800-MYFEELS. The National Council on Problem

Feeling seeks to help those needing information about feeling problems. Problem feeling is a common but chronic mental disorder and is treatable. But without help, a feeling problem may get worse. Please visit our website for more information on feeling resources in your community."

Watching him touch everything ten times before he steps out of his car, I see that Mr. Pink's problem isn't that he doesn't have feelings, it's that he has too many.

His apartment is small. Before stepping inside, he must have crunched at least a dozen crickets in the doorway. Poor bastards.

Inside, there's a sofa with scratchy pillows, a cabinet of cheap booze, and a kitchen sink full of smelly dishes. On the walls are posters of Hopper paintings. The one at the lunch counter, the one with the blonde in the shadows of a theater, and the one of the couple with the dog. I knew a collie who looked just like that one. She also lived with a couple of humans who couldn't get along. Of all the Hoppers I've seen, that one always seemed the saddest to me. That poor man is so desperate for that dog to trot over and nuzzle his hand.

I've never seen anyone, alive or not, who needed so badly to feel loved.

It's easy to miss the woods beside that house, because the people are just so damn sad. And also because that dog makes you look off to the left, to what's not on the canvas, to what she sees and hears that we can't. But those woods. I'd love to live in woods like that. They're the color of the ocean breaking on rocks. And there's a wind moving through them out of the west. It's why they, the grass, and even the fur along the neck of that collie are all bending to the right.

In Pink's bedroom, there is a narrow bed that's high enough off the floor so two Labradors stacked on top of one another could sleep under it comfortably. On the ceiling above the bed is a vintage poster of Kelly Lynch and Patrick Swayze in *Road House*.

I sit under the bed and watch Mr. Pink change. After he puts on a pair of shorts and a T-shirt, he leaves his blue jeans and sweatshirt on the floor and heads to the kitchen. That's when I notice all sorts of things on the floor: tissues, fast-food bags, old Band-Aids, cotton balls.

What a slob. I don't know how anyone can live like that. The Mustache was as tidy as they come. I sit under Mr. Pink's bed and wonder where my sweet Mustache is. Does he know I'm missing yet? Has he tried to find me? Has he called the cops and had the neighbor boy questioned?

Mr. Pink jumps in bed and says, "Call Ali." Silence. "You've reached Ali. I'm not able to take your call right now, so please leave a message." More silence.

"Ali, I know it's you. Say something!" says Mr. Pink.

"Haha, what gave it away?"

"You said 'take' instead of 'answer.' "

"What?"

"Your message is 'not able to answer your call,' not 'take your call.'"

"Aww, ratz I thought I had you that time."

"Close but no cigar. Hey, I wanted to ask you about the dishwasher."

"How was class?"

"Class, it was all right."

"Did you hear anything today from the box?" Ali said.

"Nope, still nothin'. Not a scratch or meow or anything. Do you think there really is a cat in there?"

"I dunno, probably? How would anyone know?"

"I guess the person who resets the room after the two weeks is up."

"Jeezuz, the smell, though."

"Yeah, that's the part I don't get. I mean, if there is a cat in there and it doesn't have any food or water, then there's no way it can make it to ten days . . ."

"Twelve days," Ali said. "You don't take the weekend off if you're fighting for your life."

"Or twelve days, whatever. My point is, there's no way anything can survive twelve days without food and water."

"Crocs can," Ali said.

"Crocs? No way, that's bullshit."

"It's true! I saw it somewhere that they can go up to a few months without eating."

"Months!"

"Yup, months. It even said in extreme cases they can live up to three years without food."

"Now I know you're lying."

"Look it up! It's true!"

"Okay, so, even if you're not pulling my leg and you really did read this somewhere, how would someone even know what a croc was or wasn't eating for three years?"

"I'm sure it's a croc that's tagged and monitored," Ali said.

"So you mean to tell me that in three years this croc, a croc probably living out in the Everglades or something, this croc couldn't have slipped one puny duck or fish past Joe Schmoe while he was on a piss break at the croc lab?"

"They have fancy equipment."

"Ooooh, excuse me, they have fancy equipment."

"Look, I'm not saying it's impossible, it's just what I read."

"All right, all right, so maybe the cat's alive? If there's even one in there," said Mr. Pink.

"Jeezuz, I hope not. I guess the point is you're not supposed to know. Because if you know, then that'll change how you feel about the whole thing."

"I know, I know. I'd feel like shit if I knew cats were dying in these classes."

"Sounds like someone's well on his way to getting his ES Certificate."

"We'll see. I hope the quizzes don't get hard. They've

been easy so far. Hey, I wanted to ask you about the dishwasher," said Mr. Pink.

"Here we go."

"What? I just wanted to ask you if you put dishes in it before you left my place this morning?"

"You know I did."

"Okay, so why did you put the cups in the bottom rack and not in the top?"

"Because it doesn't matter where I put them in the top rack, you're not gonna be happy."

"Come on, that's not fair," said Mr. Pink.

"You know it's true! Otherwise, why do you rearrange everything in the dishwasher after I load it? Answer me that."

"It's because there's more dishes to load, and I need the extra room."

"Uh-huh."

"Dishwasher engineers put a lot of thought into how they design the bottom and top racks. They design them so that you can get the maximum amount of dishes and pots and pans in them. Less loads means you use less energy and less water."

"You think I don't know that, dum-dum?" said Ali.

"Then why are you always getting on my ass about how I load it?"

"Me getting on your ass!? You know what, it's your dishwasher and your apartment, so how about this, you load the dishwasher and I'll empty it. How's that?"

"I can live with that."

"Is there anything else, Mr. Perfect?"

"Yeah. Will I see you tomorrow?"

"Let's play it by ear. I might have to work an extra shift."

"Okay. Good night. Hello, hello? Are you still there?"

"Yeah, I'm just fuckin' with you."

"Jeezuz, I thought you hung up on me."

"I know, haha. Get your crazy ass to bed. 'Night!" said Ali.

" 'Night."

What is Mr. Pink humming? I know that song. I think it's "I've Had the Time of My Life." Why is the bed squeaking? Oh God, I wish I was dead-dead and not just dead.

When the morning sun shines through the broken blinds of Mr. Pink's apartment, it looks even worse in the daylight than it did last night. I don't remember falling asleep at all. I'm not even sleepy now. Maybe I don't have to sleep anymore. But if I don't sleep, then I guess I won't dream, either. This whole thing is a nightmare. I wish I could wake up.

So Mr. Pink and the other four people in the lab sitting around my box don't even know whether anything is inside or not. Is this some kind of a sick joke? He said it was some sort of class, but what kind of a class is okay with killing cats? I need to figure this out, and I think I have to start with the trench-coat guy the neighbor boy gave me to. Ugh, gross: Mr. Pink is putting back on the blue jeans and sweatshirt he wore yesterday. What's he doing now? Ah, hunting for new socks, I see. Maybe there's hope for him yet.

A horn honks outside, and he starts putting his shoes on while hopping on one leg. Whoever is outside is laying on the horn like their life depends on it. Mr. Pink hustles to the front door. I better book it after him before he's gone. Even though I can probably walk through his door, that doesn't mean I'm entirely comfortable with walking through walls yet. This whole new body will take some getting used to.

The Bronco in the driveway has seen better days. The color is Bondo gray, and over the bumpers and grille are big black bars that make it look like it has a massive underbite. Driving the Bronco is a woman. She's dressed in yellow and wearing the vest everyone who works as an Emotional Support Human wears.

"Sorry I'm late, Aunt Karen."

"If ands and buts were candy and nuts, we'd all have a merry Christmas."

"I don't know what that means."

"Boy, hush."

I'm sitting in the middle of the bench seat in the back. The seats are orange, and the carpet is black. Out the window, the tall palm trees are going by and by. Where the hell are we?

"Okay, boy, now tell me, what do we do at this stoplight? What's the first step?"

"We watch for . . ."

"Stop."

"You didn't let me finish!" said Mr. Pink.

"Take that sass outta your voice and try again."

"I'm sorry. I didn't have a chance to finish what I was saying."

"I didn't need to hear the rest of what you were gonna say, because you had already missed the most important part."

"Oh, right. Being first in the empathy lane."

"Yup. Start again."

"Step one: make sure we are the first car in the empathy lane."

"Go on."

"Next, press the brake with the left foot and hover my right foot over the gas pedal."

"Where do your hands go?"

"At nine and three o'clock," said Mr. Pink.

"Good. What else?"

"Um . . . Oh, I know, I'm supposed to watch the green light for the cross traffic. As soon as it turns yellow, I'm supposed to then have one eye waiting for the red and another on the cars trying to make the light."

"And what are your feet doing at this point?"

"Right, I'm lifting my foot that's on the brake up just a little, so that when I need to hit the gas I can press down on the gas at the same time that I'm lifting my foot off the brake."

"And what's the last part?"

"The last part is, if we catch someone trying to cross after the light's turned red, we peel rubber and slam right into them."

"You got it. None of this means squat if we're not at the front of the line."

"How many people do you think you hit a day?" asked Mr. Pink.

"At intersections? Probably a half dozen. It's a big city, and many folks still think that whatever they gotta get to is more important than where everyone else is going."

"Do they get mad when you hit them?"

"Nah, they're too woozy from the crash to get their hackles up."

"So what do you do after a crash?"

"I just call Dispatch and tell them my ID, the type of crash, and the address. So I might say, 'K-Dawg calling in a T-bone at Alameda and Third.' And that's it. Then you just wait for the clean-up crew to show up."

"Do you think it works?" asked Mr. Pink.

"Do I think what works?"

"Crashing into people. Does it make them slow down from that point on?"

"That ain't my department. You'd have to talk to someone who does the exit interviews six months after the crash. My job—and it'll be your job if you get that

Emotional Statistics Certificate—my job is to stop them when they're fuckin' up, to remind them that their feelings ain't the only ones that matter in this world."

So that's why Mr. Pink is taking the class. The car starts moving, and I wonder whether I've ever known anyone who liked being forced to think of others. Yeah, I'd say that's a big no. I've never understood these humans who think you can force someone else to be nice.

Why is she pulling into this parking lot?

"Is that a pity party, Aunt Karen?"

"You bet it is. Pop quiz: what gave it away?"

"Because all of the cars in the parking lot are white?"

"You tellin' me or askin' me?"

"Sorry, I mean, because all the cars in the lot are white."

"That's better. Now, why do you think I picked this lot to cruise?"

"Because at pity parties people are feeling sorry for themselves and not thinking about others?"

"Partly. Their feelings are one thing, but what they do is another. When they come out of that party, some of them are gonna pull out the wrong way from the parking space."

"How so?"

"Instead of backing out, they're gonna pull forward, because the car in front of them is gone and they figure it's easier than having to reverse, look at the camera, and look over both shoulders."

"What's wrong with that?"

"Boy, don't you know nothin'? What's wrong with it is that nobody expects a car to pull forward. So, if someone is walking along, minding their own business, trying to find their own car so they can go home to their feelings and their own families, and then—boom—some asshat pulls forward who should've been reversing, then you have a pedestrian with a blown-out knee, or worse if it's a kid."

She kept going on like this, with Mr. Pink nodding and nodding. From the back window, I could see people walking in and out of the white tent where the pity-party music was blaring. I couldn't put my finger on the music the band was playing, something about a fast car and someone named Billy. Everyone was dressed in white and wore a frown. Their faces looked like masks, only, if you took them off, you probably wouldn't like what was underneath. I could smell the food even though my window was up: cucumber sandwiches, egg rolls, pad Thai.

Someone climbed to the small stage, clinked their glass, and said, "Dear friends, friends of friends, and soon-to-be friends, thank you so much for sharing with me your pity. I can't properly express how much it means to me to truly be seen. Please be sure to visit the photo booth and drive home safe. I look forward to repaying your generosity one day, when we throw a party in honor of *your* suffering."

Mr. Pink and his aunt had traded places and were

watching a guy who had stumbled out of the tent before the speech had started. He was wearing a white T-shirt and white mesh shorts—hardly the clothes I would think someone would wear to a party, much less one about suffering. He was tall, had a beard the color of rust, and looked hesitant on his feet. He was no Michelangelo's *David,* I'll tell you that much.

"What about him, Aunt Karen?"

"Yup, he's a good one. Look at how he didn't care that the car next to him had its door open. I bet you he's gonna pull forward outta the spot. Two-foot those pedals and get ready."

"Okay. I'm nervous."

"Remember that we're doing him a favor in the long run."

The guy slid into his white Avalon and rolled his windows down. Aunt Karen turned on "Wheel in the Sky" and said, "Get your feet ready, boy."

The first few guitar licks are slow and soft. I think it's an acoustic with steel strings. Cue the snare, because the white nose of Big Red's Avalon has pulled forward. Aunt Karen says, "Punch it!" and the Bronco's tires squeal, and we fly forward. While I sink my claws into my seat, I tuck into my shell like an armadillo for the first time and tumble like a blue bowling ball toward Mr. Pink's feet as we crunch into the white car.

DAY 4 QUIZ

Choose the answer that places the sentences in the order that feels the most true to you.

1. You felt beautiful.
2. You felt like eating a pecan pie.
3. You felt like dying.
4. At this moment.

a) 2~4~3~1
b) 1~2~4~3
c) 3~2~1~4

---

1. Maybe I am replaceable.
2. Each family is an ocean.
3. This neighborhood is a hellscape.
4. And then I remember.

a) 1~3~4~2
b) 2~1~4~3
c) 3~4~1~2

---

1. You remember your first kiss.
2. You remember your favorite sandwich.
3. You remember you can't eat dairy.
4. And you weep because.

a) 3~1~4~2
b) 2~4~3~1
c) 2~3~4~1

---

1. In a dream, you were a salad.
2. People you knew kept dying.
3. A party of five tipped you 10%.
4. Love is like that.

a) 3~2~1~4
b) 2~1~3~4
c) 1~3~2~4

Am I dead? Maybe I should open my eyes. No, maybe just one eye.

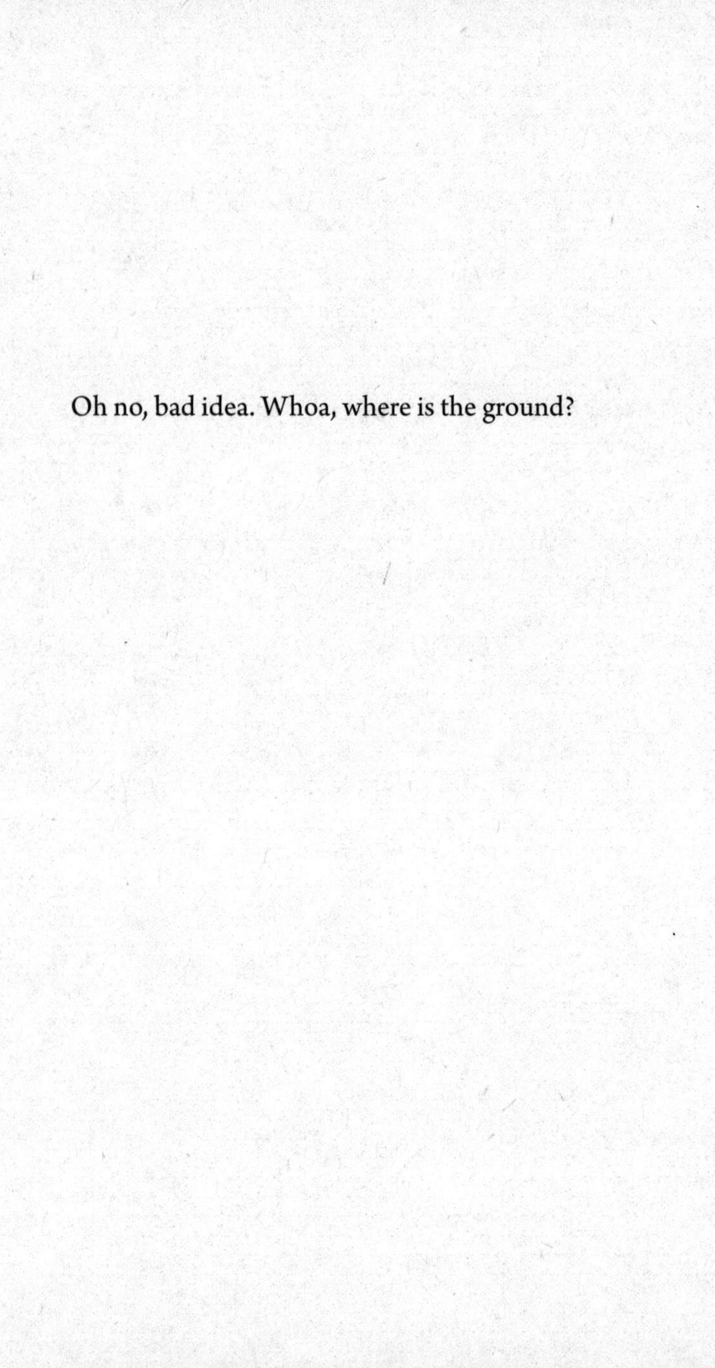

Oh no, bad idea. Whoa, where is the ground?

Everything is orange. But nothing is orange, because there's nothing here but me.

Is this heaven? Hell?

Maybe I'm dreaming, and if I keep my eyes shut, I'll wake up in the Bronco with Mr. Pink and Aunt Karen.

What's that sound? And that smell?

I'm on the floorboard of someone's car, but it's not the Bronco. I crawl up toward the window.

I think that's . . . it can't be . . . that sound is Steve Perry, and that's Aunt Karen's Bronco coming for us.

Shit, tuck!

I'm in the orange place again.

Did I time-travel? How in the hell did I do that?

And what is this place, some sort of orange bridge between here and everywhere else?

Am I still in the Bronco? Or the Avalon?
Oh jeez, what if I’m in both?

I don't like this. Being back in the box would almost be better than this orange limbo.

What's that smell? The orange place smells like flowers, and this is most definitely not flowers. I'll just peek with one eye. I can do this.

Oh no, the smell is me. Not me me, but in-the-box me. I gotta get out of here. If I can tuck into a ball and go anywhere I want, I should at least go somewhere fun, where I'm not in a box decomposing, or about to be smashed by a maniac in a Bronco.

Is this Delft?

I smell dirt. I've never left the country, much less traveled to Holland, but I didn't expect it to be dark and dirty like this. I'm afraid to untuck completely. I know Vermeer had money problems, but I thought he lived in his momma-in-law's swanky castle.

I feel like I landed in someone's filthy pocket.

Maybe I can only go so far back in time?

If I can't have the real Vermeer, let me try for Colin Firth. I'd watch him on set pretend to paint a pearl earring on Scarlett Johansson all day long.

Ratz, dirt again.

What's that sound?

And is that leather I smell?

I know this place. I'm under an old toolshed. Above me is a wood floor that's seen better days. And above that is a small closet in the back of the shed. In that closet is an old brown saddle covered in spiderwebs. It's too small for a full-grown horse, but a Shetland pony would do.

In the other room of the shed, the big room, there's rusty cans of nails and screws and washers. The smell of fresh-cut grass comes from the lawn mower that sits next to a shovel, a rake, and a pickax.

Behind the shed, you can walk out to a quiet road that bends. You cross this small bending road and the grass and weeds are twice as tall as any neighborhood cat. The only sign of you anyone will see as you walk is the tip of your tail, if you hold it up high. And if you don't, then the parting grass is the only sign you're there.

You and the grass climb a hill, and then it slopes down quickly into a small dry valley where nothing grows. Railroad tracks pass through here.

I used to sit on those tracks, nudging pennies a little at a time until each one slid off the rail. When summer was on its way out, the trains passing through the valley would make a sound that said cold was coming. Those metal cars bit the rails the way winter bites the tips of my ears.

I look out from under the shed and watch the grass moving across the road. I don't know why I still care about whether someone can see me or not, and what they would think about seeing a green cat with a blue armadillo shell. It's not like anyone can see me.

I sit here for what feels like forever. I know what's behind me at the other end of the shed. I hear it before I see it. And I smell it before I hear it.

It's my momma.

And it's me.

I can hear my squeaks. I've just been born, and my eyes aren't even open yet. But my little black-and-pink toes have claws, and with those claws I find my momma's milk.

Am I still the Cat of Christmas Past if I don't go look at the kitten that was me, or *is* me, cuddled with my momma, and purring like I didn't have a care in the world because I didn't?

Our days living under this shed were good ones. There were plenty of mice in the field across the road, hardly any children around to bother us. Only one dog they called Blackie, who was ferocious, but only with other dogs. The retired couple in the house kept him around because he loved cats but hated anything that barked.

At night, they would have dinner, watch the early news, and then watch new episodes of *Singing School,* their favorite TV show. Blackie would crawl under the shed with us and cover his ears for a whole hour.

Long before I was born, humans had stopped using bloodhounds to hunt for people who were trapped in buildings that had collapsed. Instead, humans were used for that job now. They underwent some sort of special training; I don't know the details. The point is, humans had replaced bloodhounds in all the old jobs they used to do. Humans didn't just sniff around at accident sites. They were also tracking the scents of criminals, as well as going on hunts for deer and duck and whatnot.

Humans had bred bloodhounds to be Liam Neeson from one of the Mustache's favorite movies. They possessed a very particular set of skills, skills honed over long careers, skills that made bloodhounds a nightmare for anyone whose scent they got a hold of.

Humans developing these skills in their own species, and thus taking over these jobs, meant that suddenly all these bloodhounds were unemployed. Sure, some of them tried guarding banks or herding sheep, but they weren't any good at it. What's more, op-eds started cropping up calling bloodhounds "lazy," "mongrels," and accusing them of "taking our jobs."

Hollywood came to the rescue and produced *Singing*

School, a show that gathered those bloodhounds. Or, at least, gathered the bloodhounds that had any kind of talent for karaoke.

Every week, that black-and-tan chorus would moan, in the way that only bloodhounds can moan, all the top forty hits of the week.

Those were good days. Food, shelter, love. We had plenty of all three. Life seemed so simple back then.

I miss my momma.

I can't crawl the five feet behind me to go see her. What if I see myself as a kitten that's just been born, and then something weird happens and we melt together or disappear completely? Isn't there some law of physics about how the same matter can't occupy the same space or something like that? If I think things are bad now, they'd surely be worse if I turned into some sort of gray goop. Not to mention the heart attack it'd give my poor momma!

But am I even still the same me? Wouldn't being some sort of half cat, half armadillo change the rules somehow? I bet Sir Isaac Newton never accounted for something like me in all his calculations.

Back in the place of orange flowers. Even if no other place is for me, this place is.

At least, I think it is.

At least, when I wake up here, I still look the same and feel the same. Even if I'm still getting used to what it's like to look and feel this way.

There's no above or below here. No ground or sky to pull my body around.

This orange world could be a giant flower petal, for all I know. A petal so long and wide that it's my entire universe.

And what would that make me, a weird insect?

No, an insect eats and sleeps and shits. I don't do any of that. I just float here. Is thinking enough to actually be alive? Isn't eating and shitting more important than thought?

I hunger, therefore I am.

The journey of a thousand hungers begins with one bite.

That which does not kill us makes us hungrier.

Hunger is what happens when you're busy making other hungers.

You must be the hunger you wish to see in the world.

You only hunger once, but if you do it right, once is enough.

Hungry times never last, but hungry people do.

'Tis better to have hungered and lost than to have never hungered at all.

A hunger is but what it knows.

I came, I saw, I hungered.

Hunger is power.

In three words I can sum up everything I've learned about hunger: it goes on.

Hunger is grace under pressure. *Y pues nada y nada,* as that great lover of cats Old Papa Hemingway wrote.

Nada grant me the serenity to accept the nada I cannot change, courage to change the nada I can, and the wisdom to know the difference, living one nada at a time; enjoying one nada at a time; taking this nada as it is and not as I would have it; trusting that nada will make all things right if I surrender to nada; so that I may be reasonably happy in this nada and supremely happy with nada forever in the next.

DAY 5 QUIZ

Cross out the sentence that is the most unrelated to the rest.

1. You loved me.
2. Tyson bit off some of Holyfield's ear.
3. Your brain was shaped like a boxing glove.
4. We loved each other.
5. I was shaped like a punching bag.

---

1. I wanted to make beautiful bonsai.
2. I had all the tools.
3. You slapped me hard.
4. A tree will do anything to reach the light.
5. We ran out of words.

---

1. I never saw anyone make you smile like that.
2. She married an old flame.
3. You shaved and smelled like cinnamon.
4. It must've been love.
5. I never saw anyone make you cry like that.

---

1. You drew Jesus on a handkerchief.
2. Another birthday came and went.
3. You made a belt buckle with my initials.
4. You were the healthiest I'd ever seen.
5. I misread Inmate Correspondence as Intimate Correspondence.

Saturdays have a feel. The Mustache taught me this when he would sleep in on Saturdays. It was nice to stay curled behind his knees long after the sun had come up and morning birds had flown off to start their day. I felt lucky because, while those birds were having another day just like the one before and the one that would come after, I had something different.

Sometimes the Mustache would even leave the bed before me. On those days, he'd sneak off but first slide a pillow under the quilt so that I wouldn't notice his legs were gone. The quilt had been his abuelo's and was over fifty years old. He took such good care of it that it was in better shape than some quilts I've seen that aren't even a year old.

The back of it and the edges were the color of beet root, and the top was made of different squares of fabric. Some squares were fuzzy, while others were rough. I loved the corduroy ones best. And how the whole thing was a mishmash of colors that all somehow came together to make something pretty.

On the Saturdays when I'd sleep in, I'd chirp when I

jumped off the bed, because I knew what I'd find in the living room. Right on schedule, there would be the Mustache eating a bowl of atole and hunched over a chessboard. What woke me up was the smell of the pecans, raisins, and agave in the atole. The scent would drift into my nose while I was sleeping. The smell would always pull me awake from the same dream I had every Friday night.

I'm sitting on a pink velour desk chair. The legs are gold and the back has the most perfectly folded pleats you've ever seen. In the room, people I don't know are shooting what I think is a movie.

There's a living room with a low couch. Low coffee table and TV stands, too. The perfect height for senior cats to jump up on.

There are cameras and giant lights. A man always yells the same thing, in a voice as thick as pudding, from a back room: "Where's the dead cat? Someone go to the truck and bring me a cover for this microphone."

Then the dream ends.

I don't know why I would dream this on Friday nights. I blame the cube of cheddar the Mustache would give me for my Friday-night treat. I always liked to think that if the dream had continued I would've turned out to be the star of the movie they were shooting.

Instead, I would peek out of the Mustache's bedroom and watch him puzzling over a chess problem he had set up. When he was a kid, his dad had taught him to play chess. They played together for five years before the little Mustache finally won his first game.

But before then, his dad would make the Mustache take his queen off the board before a game. Or his bishops. The idea was to teach him how to use his other pieces better. No surprise, then, that the Mustache came to love strategy, grew into the kind of person who would study a decision from every angle, talk out all the scenarios, and then make a choice. He did this with everything, from how to pay off a loan to how to cook the perfect boiled egg.

I saw him try to boil an egg so many different ways. Eventually, he settled on ten minutes in the pan. Then right to an ice bath. After twenty minutes, he'd take it out. The shell would fall clean off. Then he'd put the egg in a mug, sprinkle salt and pepper over it, cover it with his hand, and tumble that egg around until it was coated. Add a small piece of ham steak, and this was his breakfast Monday through Friday.

When the Mustache sees me peeking out of his bedroom with my sleepy eyes, he walks to my food dish and calls me over.

Now that I'm awake, he slips the needle onto "On and On." It's been our Saturday-morning song so long, I can't remember what our song was before he brought home Curtis Harding's *Face Your Fear* record.

I eat my breakfast while the drums and bass guitar fill the house with that warm feeling you get when you step into the sunlight on the first day of spring. And don't get me started on the trombone. That horn cuts through the air like a train made of solid gold on its way to heaven.

After the Harding record finishes, it's the James Jamerson tribute morning. And afternoon. And sometimes even into the night. "Bernadette," "For Once in My Life," "What's Going On," "My Girl," "You Can't Hurry Love," and "I Heard It Through the Grapevine" all making our house swell, but not with words, like you would think, because these versions of the songs didn't have lyrics. They had been removed, the recordings re-released as part of the James Jamerson centenary.

It really says something that people would celebrate the bass in this way, the backbone not just of songs, but of the heart in every living thing.

Those were our Saturdays. And Sundays we did less, even if the days still felt full of love and stillness and the kind of slow light that traveled so far to reach you, never in a hurry, always arriving at the time it was always meant to.

It's growing dark outside. But inside, this room, this building, is still humming with energy. I can feel the past lives that walked on these floors.

There's the donut shop with the baker who had hairy knuckles, ten years ago. Her laugh was like a thunderhead.

An acupuncturist worked here five years before that.

He made humans into hedgehogs, and his car had one tire with a slow leak.

Long before them, this was an art gallery. There were fewer walls and copper popsicles that hung from the ceilings.

I wonder what the students are doing right now? Are they at home, or just getting ready to prowl through the night for fun and trouble? And what do their homes look like? If something breaks in their house, can they fix it, or do they call someone?

The Mustache knew his way around a toolbox. He liked to do things with his hands. He also didn't like it when other people touched his machines. When he was a kid, his grandfather had told him that he never let anyone drive his truck because a machine knows when its owner isn't behind the wheel. All it takes is one person with a heavy foot to mess up your brakes or to shred your gears. The Mustache had taken this to heart, and so he never let anyone so much as even touch his lawn mower.

It was the old kind that ran on gas. When it needed to be cleaned, we would sit on the back porch. I'd watch him remove the spark plug and turn the mower upside down. Then he'd scrape off the chunks of grass stuck to the bottom. They'd peel away like squares of green cheese. Green like me, come to think of it. I wonder, if someone saw me, if they would think that I was made of clumps of grass clippings.

What's that sound?

It's like two dimes being rubbed together.

There it is again.

Someone is jiggling the doorknob to the classroom. Who could it be at this hour, and what could they possibly want from an empty room?

Well, I guess it's not really empty, because I'm here, both inside and outside the box.

Shoot, the door is opening. Tuck!

Orangeville, USA. I forgot tucking into my shell would land me back here in flower land. What am I afraid of?

I know I can't be harmed here, but can anyone hurt me back in the world? Isn't it a requirement that something has to be able to see you in order to hurt you? And if I'm invisible, then I should be safe.

But if I'm safe in my blue shell with my long green legs, what about my other body? Wasn't there a movie where a guy's corpse was cut and he could feel the pain as a ghost?

Maybe I'm making that up. But still, I need to check on my body in the box.

I have to go back.

She's wearing a ski mask, but I know she's a young woman. I can smell the generations of struggle on her. The lungs of a great-grandfather in the coal mines. An auntie with fibroids. A father who never gave a damn. An elementary-school heartbreak.

What's she doing?

I can't believe she's knocking on the box. If I was still alive in there, she would've given me a heart attack.

Einstein forgot to turn the ringer off on her phone. It's clear she's no professional. I mean, who wears a ski mask during a break-in?

"I told you not to call me."

Wait a minute. I know that voice, but from where exactly?

"Yes, I'm inside the building already."

It's Mr. Pink! This has to be Ali. Mr. Pink's girlfriend. What is she up to?

"Yes, the building is empty. I'm sure of it. I looked in every room. I'm at the box. Let me put the phone down and put you on speaker."

“Do you see any kind of lock or door on the box? Ali? Can you hear me?”

“I can hear you. I don’t see any kind of door.”

“Are there seams?”

“Seams? I didn’t know you were taking a sewing class.”

“Haha, you know what I mean. Where the walls are put together.”

“Try again. Any other ideas?”

“Can you lift it?”

“Nope. It’s bolted to the table somehow.”

“Look under the table, then! Do you see any bolts, or anything coming through? Ali?”

“Hold your horses, I’m looking. Nope. There’s nothing under there except for a lot of bubble gum and dust.”

“Gross.”

“Any other ideas, babe?”

“Try turning the table over. Do you want me to come in and help?”

“No, no, keep the car running. If you get caught, you’ll be kicked out of the class.”

“Okay.”

“So—turn it over? That’s not a bad idea. What if there really is a cat in there and it’s still alive?”

“Can a cat even survive this long?”

“If they put food and water in there, then I don’t see why not?”

“If there is a cat in there, we have to get it out. Or at

least call the animal-cruelty hotline, or someone at the local news station."

I have to get back in that box. Maybe I can let them know I'm in there somehow.

"If there's a cat inside, it could be scared to death, or starving, or both. Ali, try saying, 'Here, kitty, kitty.' It's the universal message for 'Hey, I wanna be your friend.'"

"Here, kitty, kitty."

"Anything, babe?"

"Nothing. Wait, I think I heard something. It's faint."

"Is it a meow?"

"No, it's not an animal sound. It's something else. It sounds like glass being scratched."

"Shit—there's supposed to be a glass vial of radiation or something in the box with the cat."

"Are you serious?"

"Ali, get out of there. What if that stuff leaks out?"

"But what about the cat?"

"If it's scratching the container for the radiation, then it's a goner."

"This is so messed up."

"Get out now. For all we know, they have a way to monitor when the radiation thing breaks."

"Okay, fine. I'll see you in a sec."

If Mr. Pink and Ali are asking questions, then maybe someone else will, too. Maybe, if someone else comes poking around, the Mustache will hear something and find me.

I'll never forget the look on his face after I went missing for a few days. When a cat goes missing, it's not for the reasons you think. It's not because we have some other family we live with and we've forgotten about you. And it's not that we're off on some extended hunt, decimating the neighborhood mouse population. It's not even about sex.

Some humans refer to it as the call of the wild. I never liked that phrase. It makes it sound like we're not still wild on your couch and in your bed and in the cardboard box you set out for us to sit in.

It's more like a pilgrimage. And by that I don't mean we're traveling very far. I've known some cats who've put in miles and miles while they were gone, and others who were never more than a single block away from home.

It's a pilgrimage, and the destination is blood. A dog can spend its whole life inside, eating kibble and wet food, and though it may wish it had something different to eat, it'll never have the same need rise up in the pit of its spirit, a need that compels it to go outside and spend a few days finding its own food.

I don't mean scavenging. Any stray can do that. No, I mean stalking, observing, and killing a bird or a mouse or whatever looks tasty. But just killing something isn't enough to make the need go away. No, we have to eat what we killed, just as our ancestors did before us. Tear the fur from the flesh and then the flesh from the bone. Feel the warm meat between our lips as the body that just a few minutes before was flying or swimming or jumping grows cold. Lick our paws and clean the blood from our faces.

In this way, we honor our place in the world. This is how we survive living inside, away from the wind and grass and trees that are as much a part of us as we are a part of them.

The price to live with you is blood. It doesn't matter if we are a purebred Himalayan or a shelter rescue who never knew its parents. When we don't pay this price, then things get bad.

Couches get torn.

Arms get scratched.

Closets get peed in.

Sleep gets interrupted.

And when it's really bad, we even lick our own fur off. The Friday night when I was pacing in the window for an hour, the Mustache let me go outside, even though it was late. He probably hoped some night air would make me feel better.

The weekend I was gone hunting, I never forgot about him completely. But the memory of him did grow small. Small like the stars next to the moon. I pushed his memory deep inside of me. It sat there quietly, in the dark, until it was time to go home.

Mr. Pink looks like he has a case of the Mondays.

I wonder what he's thinking, just sitting there with the other students, watching the box that I'm decomposing in? Is he thinking about his aunt Karen and how, after he completes this class, he'll be able to drive his own beat-up truck and smash into people's cars to teach them a lesson about kindness?

Maybe the job wouldn't bother him at all? Maybe he's one of those people who when they pass a wreck on the road don't even look, they just keep driving. Isn't it natural to want to look, to gawk, and to see what happened?

When a cat is hit by a car, we don't just walk by and pretend like they're not there.

Our ears tell us the stiffness of their hair by the sound of a breeze passing through it. Our nose tells us how dry the organs are, and how little water is left in their skin. Our eyes tell us what tribe they came from, and what was the last thing they saw, and what the light was like as it faded in their eyes. And our nose, when it touches their nose, it tells us what it feels like to become something else, something beyond what our mommas knew.

I've touched plenty of warm, dry noses of cats that were dead, but none of those times ever prepared me for this.

The cat tribes have lots of different stories about how the world began and how we got here and where everything comes from, but never any stories about a cat taking on the parts of another animal. Or changing color. Or time-traveling!

This is crazy.

Mr. Pink's leg is bouncing like a cricket. He's nervous. Maybe he's worried someone saw him and Ali drive away from here. Or maybe he knows I'm dead inside that box. I wonder if any of these fools know that a cat can't live without food or water for more than three days. If they know that, then they sure as hell gotta know that I was never walking outta that box at the end of their class.

How do they live with themselves?

Maybe that's what the class is about, living with yourself when you see people do messed-up things. No cat ever needed to take a class to learn how to do that. Cruelty happens all the time, and sometimes you're the one doing it. It is what it is, as my momma used to say.

Where's this guy with the mop of blond hair going? The class isn't over yet. The bell hasn't rung, and no one else is packing up their desk. I'm gonna see what he's up to.

. . .

Figures Blondie would drive a car that drives itself. I'm so glad the Mustache never bought one of these death traps. Whoever thought humans should have fewer hands on the wheel was an idiot.

Blondie tells the radio to turn on, and a voice from the ceiling of the car says, "Would you like to hear your favorite station?"

Blondie says yes, and two voices come on, talking about the war.

Traffic is slow. A woman driving a car with only three tires pulls up beside us. The car is the color of a sparrow and has two tires in front and one in the back. The roof and sides are open. It's more like a wheelbarrow with an engine than it is a car. She's dressed in yellow and wearing silver goggles that sparkle, with a white strap pulled tight against her long black hair. There's no way to avoid the sun in a contraption like that.

I guess Blondie got bored with the talk about the war, because he's fast asleep. The palm trees go by and by. They stand as if they're guarding something. Underneath one of them is a red billboard advertising a shooting range. There's a woman on her stomach aiming one of those machine guns that's so big it has a little kick stand in the front under the barrel. She's wearing dark-blue jeans, a black shirt, and cowboy boots. Her brown hair is in a ponytail, and she's got on goggles, and a gold belt of bullets goes from the gun to the floor and then around her waist. What a world.

Blondie's seat begins to vibrate, and the voice from earlier says, "Incoming call." Blondie wakes up and answers, "Hey."

"Hey, darling. Are you out of class?"

"Yup. I left early, remember?"

"Oh yes. How's the drive going? Were you sleeping? You sound groggy."

"Yeah, I was trying to get some rest before I meet Bob."

"Oh, I'm so glad the two of you are spending some time together. How long has it been since you've been hunting, two years?"

"Maybe more."

"Did you remember to pack your boots with the orthotics? You don't want to have an angry blister out there."

"I packed them."

"And your ChapStick? Do you have ChapStick?"

"I don't need ChapStick."

"Oh, but your lips get so dry. And you'll be out in the open in all that salt air."

"I'll be fine."

"Well, maybe Bob will have some ChapStick. I bet Sharon slipped some into his bag. Ask him for some if you feel your lips getting dry, darling."

"They won't, but I will if they do."

"How was class?"

"It was fine."

"Any movement in the box?"

"It's bolted down. It can't move."

"Oh yes, I know, but the cat inside could still bump against the walls, and if it did, I know you'd hear it because you have such great hearing."

"Nothing bumped against the walls. It's been the same since the class started. Just a whole lotta nothin'."

"Well, as long as you're feeling something and answering the questions on the quizzes honestly, I'm sure you'll get a good grade by the end of it all. You always got such good grades in college without having to study like the rest of us."

"That was a long time ago."

"Do you have enough snacks?"

"Yeah."

"Okay, so we'll see you tomorrow after class, then?"

"Yeah."

"Have fun hunting, darling."

"I will. Mostly, it'll just be nice to be outside. I feel like I never get out of the house anymore."

"Well, that'll all change when you finish this class and get your certificate."

"We'll see."

"Do you think you'll get in the water while you're out there?"

"Are you kidding? That water is always freezing!"

"I read that an ice bath reduces inflammation, soothes muscles, increases energy, and elevates a person's mood."

"You sound like an ice-bath salesman."

"Oh, I'm just telling you what I read, dear."

"I'm getting close. I gotta go."

"Okay, darling, have a blast! Please give Bob a hug for me."

"I will."

"I love you."

"Love you, too."

The car pulled up to a parking lot that was empty except for a black truck. Blondie grabbed a bag from the trunk and started walking toward the beach.

The sand is the color of bones that've been in the sun for too long. The beach is so deep and wide that you can't see the ocean. All you see when you look out in the direction of the water is sand that goes all the way to the horizon. And, from above, the sky comes down to meet it, and it's the color of these light-blue chicken eggs I saw one time. And cotton balls. Put those together, cotton balls and blue chicken eggs, and you have the sky today.

I can tell by the smell of the sand and the little creatures crawling around in it that where we're walking used to be underwater. As long as I've been alive, the ocean has been pulled back to where it's at now. Probably happened long before even my momma was born.

There's not a single thing on the beach except for a building the color of ripe tomatoes. It's more of a single room than it is a building. The roof isn't sharp, like most roofs. It's kind of like an upside-down smile. But the building does have a roof, and a window framed in white. It has two red wheels made of wood, and it sits on a green frame with green handles. It's like a cross between a rickshaw and an outhouse.

"Bob! You in there, Bob?"

"Yo, I'm here!"

"Damn, it's good to see you, man. How you been?"

"I'm good, good, brother. How 'bout you?"

"I'm doin' all right. Just glad to be out here again, finally. You see any bucks yet?"

"Nah, not yet, but I only put the feed out a couple hours ago. Come on in and change up!"

While Blondie was changing into clothes that were the same color as the sand and the sky, I sniffed around.

"You get rid of the old deer blind, Bob?"

"Yeah. The salt had eaten up the wood. I was looking around for something new and found this sucker at an antique fair in Germany. It's called a bathing machine and is from way back."

"No shit?"

"The guy who sold it to me said it was a portable changing room for women to get in and out of their bathing suits at the beach."

"Wow."

"If a lady was bashful enough, it could be rolled all the way into the water so she could be in the water without anyone seeing her."

"That hardly makes any sense."

"I'm just telling you what the dude said. He also said some shit about how the wood won't rot because it came from trees that grow near the ocean. I dunno—at some point I stopped listening and started trying to figure out how to get this bad boy back here."

"You want some cheese?"

"You know I do! I thought you couldn't eat cheese."

"I usually don't, but this is special cheese."

"If it's made out of soy, I don't want it. You know I don't eat that shit."

"It's not made out of soy, you goofball. It came from a cow. My cow, actually."

"Excuse me? When did you get a cow?"

"Remember how Barbara and I went to Italy last summer? Well, while we were there, I decided to try an experiment and eat anything that was put in front of me."

"What did you think was gonna happen?"

"Well, I thought that maybe cheese and dairy stuff over there wouldn't sit in my stomach like a rock the way it does over here because Italy has those Old World cows that they don't pump full of food that the government has souped up with chemicals. Yessir, those Italy cows eat grass that's real grass."

"So what happened?"

"I was fine!"

"You're kidding."

"Hand to God."

"So you ate pasta and desserts and drank glasses of milk and everything?"

"I didn't drink milk—I couldn't bring myself to be that crazy—but I did eat all the rest. I couldn't believe it. I felt normal for the first time in I don't know how long because I didn't have to ask the waiter what was in anything. I just ordered, ate my food, and went about my life without feeling sick."

"Sounds incredible."

"I just couldn't stop thinking about how crazy this all was, so I asked the waitress if she knew where they bought their dairy from. She gave us the address of a farm near Gubbio, so we drove out there one weekend. You won't believe what we found."

"Let me guess: were they hugging the cows once per hour?"

"Ha! No, smart ass, they weren't. What shocked us was that the dairy farm had a contract with the police academy. And not just this one—all the dairy farms in the country have one."

"Police?"

"Yeah. Turns out that for the last part of the police training the academy sends the recruits to dairy farms, where a recruit will sit with one cow for a year."

"Now I know those Italians have gone off their rockers."

"It's wild, man. Each recruit will keep a diary for the year. In it they'll write about their life and the cow's life."

"What happens at the end of the year?"

"They graduate and become cops."

"That's the craziest thing I've ever heard."

"You can't argue with the results, though. Not only is the milk comin' out of those cows healthier than anything we got over here, but police shootings in Italy are down to almost zero."

"That's wild."

"No kidding. I told Barbara halfway through our trip that I was gonna buy one of these Italian cows, because when we got back home I couldn't just go back to the way things were."

"Tell me you didn't."

"I did."

"You crazy bastard, I can't believe you bought a cow and had it shipped all the way here!"

"She's a big one, too."

"They're all big! Do you milk it?"

"Hell, no. I mean, I learned how, but I let Barbara do it."

"Okay, here's what I don't get. If what the cows are fed in Italy is what makes the difference in their milk, then why didn't you just have the food they eat shipped here from Italy to feed to American cows? Wouldn't that have been less of a pain in the ass?"

"I see where you're going with this, but that wouldn't work."

"Why not? Explain it to me, Mr. Cow Scientist."

"You see, you need a cow that's not only been eating what they got in Italy from the time it was born, but also one that's been drinking their water. And you know their waters are gonna be different than our water. Plus, when the cows are babies . . ."

"Calves."

"What?"

"Baby cows are called calves."

"All right, Bill Nye. Stop interrupting."

"Okay, okay, I'm just saying."

"So, when the cows are calves, the calves are drinking their mothers' milk. And what have their mothers been eating and drinking all their lives?"

"Italian grass and water."

"Bingo! Giving an American cow Italian food and water wouldn't erase all the fucked-up shit it's been given to eat and drink its whole life. You could feed them filet mignon and it wouldn't make a difference."

"Filet mignon?"

"What?"

"You can't feed steak to a cow!"

"Why not?"

"Because it's against the laws of nature, you sick bastard."

"Come on, pigs will eat other pigs if given half a chance. And don't give me any of this bullshit about how a cow is a higher life form, because everyone knows pigs are the smartest animals on a farm."

"You're too much. I don't know anyone who loves fettuccine Alfredo enough to buy a whole damn cow from Italy and have it shipped across the ocean."

"What else am I gonna spend my money on?"

"I need to try some of that fancy cheese."

"We better get quiet if we want any bucks to come near this grain pile. Did you bring the bullets?"

"Yeah. I had a helluva time getting them. I had to ask a guy who knows a guy, but I got them. They don't make many derringer bullets anymore."

"Shells."

"What?"

"They're called shells, not bullets."

"So you're a bullet scientist now? And besides, you're the one who called them bullets in the first place!"

"I'm just saying, words matter. Can I see them?"

"Here. I could only get two."

"They're heavier than I thought they'd be."

"Where did you find the gun?"

"It belonged to Barbara's grandpa. She doesn't like guns, and never goes in the safe, so she won't notice it's gone."

"I can't believe you're actually gonna shoot it. I've never known a dude who actually shot a gun, much less shot it at something."

"I'll only shoot it if I have to. It's a single-shot pistol. I have my knife. You got yours?"

"Of course. You know, you'll probably have to get

really close for that gun to do anything to a buck. If you don't, you'll probably just piss it off."

"I know, I know. Quit being such a nag. Okay, now shut your trap and let's see what comes our way."

I jumped to the top of their blind, closed my eyes, and listened to the waves that I couldn't see. I think the Mustache would like it out here. Not for the hunting—he couldn't hurt a fly. In fact, I've seen him whisper to flies that were trapped inside, stuff like, "It's okay. I won't hurt you," and then they would let him pick them up by the wing with his fingers and carry them outside of the house. No, I think the Mustache would like the peace and quiet.

There's no moon tonight, and the sky is cloudy. I hear a buck breathing somewhere far out there. I can feel his warm breath moving through the chilly air. I can even feel his heart thumping inside of him. I can tell he's no spring chicken, because he's taking his time getting here to the pyramid of food on the beach. The growl in his stomach tells me that he'd like to get here sooner. He's right to be careful. He probably has a family who depends on him not just to help them find food, but to protect them with that massive rack of antlers.

I can't believe Blondie and Bob are gonna try and kill him. And for what? They don't need the food if they're buying buildings and cows in other countries and having them shipped here. They're the opposite of hungry people.

He's getting closer.

One hoof at a time.

He's flicking his tail.

He's still too far away for them to make him out in the dark.

Maybe I can scare him off. I have to try.

Big surprise: I don't like the feel of sand between my toes now that I'm dead any more than I did when I was alive.

He's not moving. Is he looking at me? I'm close enough so he must be. He must be terrified, seeing a long green cat with a blue armadillo shell on the beach. I bet he's wondering if he ate the wrong mushrooms at the dunes on his way over here.

I don't wanna traumatize the poor thing, so I'll just sit here and wash my face.

He has one leg up.

His rack is so massive and wide it looks like he has an upside-down umbrella attached to his head. Okay, big boy, now's the time. Stomp a few times to let everyone know there's danger ahead, and then turn back.

Wait, what's he doing? Why is he walking this way? Doesn't he see me sitting here?

Shoot, he can't see me.

Maybe he can hear me, then.

That's the loudest growl I got, and he's still coming. Damn it.

He's handsome as hell. His backside looks like the

cutest miniature moon just dancing in the dark. I once knew a cat who partnered up with a horse. If I was five years younger and still alive . . .

I gotta get back to Blondie and Bob. I feel like I could run through this dark forever and never run out of beach. I wonder, if I went in the water, if I would float. Or drown, for that matter.

There they are.

They're not even hiding.

They can see the buck, and the buck can see them, too. He's just standing there and has a look on his face that I've seen before. Last time I saw it was on a tomcat, years ago, when I still lived under the deck, before I met Lucky Charms. That tomcat had been around the block a few times and had won more than his fair share of fights. He had the same look on his face as this buck, the look that says, "You're on my turf and this is my food, so get out or get hurt."

The only thing that old tom didn't figure was my being a momma, and how I wasn't fighting to put food in just one belly, but in three.

Blondie's knife is out.

The buck has lowered his head.

I can't believe Blondie is charging the buck. He's got grit, I'll give him that.

Blondie has slipped, and now the buck's on top of him. Oh God, he's pinned Blondie's shoulder to the sand with his horns. Where the fuck is Bob? The smell of piss coming from the crotch of Bob's pants tells me he's not gonna be any help.

Wait, what is that in Blondie's other hand? Oh no, it's the gun.

Blondie points it at the buck's head and then I hear rattle out of my throat a hiss louder than I've ever heard before.

Blondie turns, looks me dead in the eye, and I swear he sees me, because he swings the gun and points it right at me as the buck rears up on its hind legs and drops his head down with all his weight.

Flowers.

Orange flowers. And the smell of hay after a summer rain.

DAY 6 QUIZ

Choose the word that best completes the sentence.

1. I wish we still celebrated __________ in this country.
   a. Thanksgiving
   b. Christmas
   c. Halloween

2. I wish restaurants still had ________ on the menu.
   a. chicken
   b. fish
   c. lamb

3. ________ all the years I've worked, I feel young and vibrant.
   a. In spite of
   b. Because of
   c. Forget

4. I wholeheartedly _______ the new law that says a doppelgänger can contest your will.
   a. applaud
   b. resist
   c. question

5. The one big regret of my childhood is that I _______ shared my lunch with the kid who identified as a possum.
   a. always
   b. never
   c. halfheartedly

If no one's gonna sit at Blondie's desk, I might as well. It's different, seeing the box my poor body is rotting in from one of these chairs.

I swear Blondie looked me dead in the eye when I hissed. I wonder if he made it off that beach last night. Whatever that buck did to him, Blondie had it comin'.

If I get angry enough, can people see me? Am I like Patrick Swayze in *Ghost*? Only he never changed color and turned into some sorta beast, like I have. I'm pretty sure that makes me even Swayzier than Swayze.

Now, who is this silver fox? I've never seen her before. I like her shoes. They're like part sock, part shoe. It's exactly the kind of shoe a cat would wear if we wore shoes. Nice job on the colors, too. I count at least three—no, four. Wait, five colors if you count the white background. Rust, basil, violet, lemon. I wonder if she knows that those are jungle colors, that if she was walking through a jungle in the middle of the day, her feet would be perfectly camouflaged so that she'd look like she was just floating on air. Like a ghost.

I know she's not a student. She doesn't have the same

scent as them. She smells like a mix of boredom and desperation.

"Good morning, everyone. Just pretend I'm not here. One of your classmates suffered a fatal accident and won't be returning, so I'm just going to remove his desk and then skedaddle. Just pretend like I'm not here."

Being carried around on a chair while other people watch is downright regal. I could get used to this.

"Oh, I almost forgot to remind all of you. You are now past the halfway point of the course. You have four more days remaining. Good luck, and happy feeling!"

The door closes behind us. She carries the desk down a hallway that is way too bright and talks to herself.

"'Happy feeling'? I wish no one had ever coined the term 'happy feeling'! At least it's better than 'merry feeling.' My happy feeling is gonna be heading north for a vacation as soon as this course is over. Harold and I talked about vacationing at the lake where they shot *The Great Outdoors,* and I'm finally doing it. I wish he was still here, God rest his soul. I know he'll be with me in spirit."

At the end of the hall, we reach a door with a keypad. I wish I could tell her that Harold won't be with her. If he was still hanging around, I'd be able to see him. And he'd probably be able to see me. Maybe Harold has turned into a purple minotaur with wings and is off having his own adventures.

"It'll be nice to take a break from offering this course, since I've run out of cats for the boxes."

I hear what she says, but I also don't hear what she says. My mind goes white, and I fall off the desk. I just sit there, in a room full of boxes exactly like the one I woke up in just a week ago. She turns off the light, closes the door, and walks out.

When she carried me down the hallway to this room, her sock shoes were as quiet as humans think mice are. But now, knowing what I know, the sound of her walking away sounds like a train rumbling by forever.

It was her. She must be the person the trench-coat guy sold me to.

It was her.

It was her all along.

I feel like puking, only there's nothing to puke, because I don't eat or drink anymore. And yet my body still goes through the motions as I dry-heave again and again. Each time I do, it feels like my face is being peeled back and off. I don't even cough up any hair balls. I still bathe myself, but it's more out of habit, because my hair stays perfect. Perfectly green cat hair.

I'm going to kill her.

But first, I need to use her to help me track down the trench-coat guy, because he's got it comin', too. If he never got involved, then I would never have been delivered into the hands of this psycho, and I would still be at home with my sweet Mustache. After I take care of these two, I have to find him.

. . .

It feels like I sat in that storeroom for weeks, when really only a couple of hours have passed. I find Silver Fox in her office, on the other side of the building. What is she eating? Smells like pretzel nuggets. Well, isn't she the picture of comfort, with her feet on her desk like she doesn't have a care in the world? That voice coming from her phone. I know that voice from somewhere. It sounds like the news the Mustache used to listen to.

While she was sitting here inhaling those nuggets, I walked through my first wall. I didn't even have to try hard. It wasn't like when Swayze tried and tried to push the bottle cap across the nasty subway platform. I didn't have a ghost to teach me how to be what I am. Maybe, if I was a human, I'd need someone to tell me what that ghost told Swayze, to say, "You can't push it with your finger! . . . It's all in your mind. . . . You think you're crouched on that floor? Bullshit! You ain't got a body no more, son!"

God, I love that scene.

I never met a cat who had to be taught how to touch something. We're born knowing how to move our bodies in ways even we can hardly believe sometimes. The Mustache used to love showing me this video of an orange tabby karate-kicking some fool German shepherd. The Mustache said millions of people watched that video over and over. I guess they thought that was really something. They didn't even know the half of it, because that wasn't news to me. It wasn't like that cat was the Bruce

Lee of cats or anything. I know a run-of-the-mill tabby when I see one.

I once saw a cat clothesline a French bulldog. The dog was the color of biscuits. It was one of those purebreds who think they're hot stuff. That stocky son of a gun was yap-yap-yapping at this tuxedo tom who was just standing there, and the next thing you know, that tom grabbed ole Frenchie by the neck, and in a black-and-white whir flipped him on his back. That dog popped up like a firecracker and hauled ass.

I wish she'd turn off her phone. Or listen to something else. I hate the news. Everyone's voice sounds exactly the same way: fake.

"Today marks day fourteen of the trial of former Police Officer Randall "Goose" Showalter, who is accused of using excessive force with a baton to take the life of an unarmed citizen. This trial has gripped the nation. Last week, when Showalter's attorney informed the court that he would testify in his own defense, it came as a shock to the public. Legal experts agreed that Showalter could only hurt his case. But today he took the stand. Our own Wendy Campbell was in the courtroom today. Wendy, can you describe for us what the atmosphere was like in the courtroom?"

"I sure can, Sonya. The air was thick with anticipation. While Judge Patel has prohibited cameras or video of the proceedings, today they allowed the room to exceed capacity so that the family of Julie Flores could attend. It was standing room only, Sonya."

"Wendy, what can you share about Showalter's first day on the stand?"

"Showalter's testimony took the courtroom by surprise, Sonya. When the defense asked Showalter if he had any pre-existing medical conditions, no one could have foreseen where the line of questioning would lead. The defense submitted into evidence lab tests that confirmed Showalter's testimony that he suffers from toxoplasmosis. When the district attorney objected and asked the relevance of this, the defense claimed the evidence would speak to the defendant's state of mind. Judge Patel allowed it, and that's when Showalter dropped a bomb and testified that the toxoplasmosis he contracted from his cat made him do it. Needless to say, the court erupted with emotion. It took Judge Patel almost five minutes to quiet the room. It was only after they threatened to clear the room that order was restored."

"In all my years on the air, Wendy, I can't say I've ever heard the "My cat made me do it" defense before."

"You're not alone, Sonya. The prosecution immediately asked for a full day's continuance in order to evaluate the evidence before they cross-examine the defendant. Judge Patel granted the prosecution's motion and said the trial would resume on Monday."

I hate that infernal bell. Maybe it'll get Silver Fox up and moving. What kind of a teacher just sits around eating snacks and watching the news all day?

I hear footsteps in the hall. And a door opening and closing. The students must be leaving.

Finally, we have signs of life! In another life, I would've walked over to those crumbs falling off her shirt and sniffed them, maybe even would've licked them for the salt. Not today, Satan. Not today.

While Silver Fox closes up the building, I'm gonna sit right here by the door and wait for her, so I can hitch a ride to her house. There has to be something there that will lead me to the trench-coat guy.

Is she really gonna sit here in this dark garage and wait for "The Piña Colada Song" to finish? Of all the driveway songs, I never imagined this would be on anyone's list. Maybe Curtis Mayfield's "Move On Up," or "Roses" by Outkast. Or even Frank's "Fly Me to the Moon." I get it, some grooves you just can't interrupt or they'll hang over the rest of your day. Like getting soaked in the rain and never drying out.

At least she had the sense to turn the car off so the exhaust doesn't kill us. Well, I guess only she would die. But not yet. I still need her.

I can't believe we made it through the front door. I couldn't understand why she didn't use the door inside the garage, but now I get it. There's a tower of newspapers in front of it. And in front of that tower, another tower. And then more towers in front and beyond and all around.

For all the mess, the newspapers are neatly stacked. I don't see a single issue anywhere that isn't perfectly lined up with the rest. She has an eye for detail, I'll give her that.

Walk in the front door and you're basically in the kitchen. The person who made that design decision must have grown up in one of those houses where the kitchen was all the way in the back of the house, so that when they came home from school hungry, they'd have to run the gauntlet of "You're home" and "How was school?" before finally making it all the way to the refrigerator.

Walk to the right from the kitchen and there's a small office area, and beyond that a large living room with a huge window. The window is even larger because the ceilings are unusually high for a house in the hills. If you walk the other way from the kitchen, then you'll find a laundry room, a bathroom, and two bedrooms.

She sits down on a couch surrounded by the newspaper towers with a plate of cold deli turkey, chickpeas, and banana chips. How does someone with as much money as her not eat something better? I guess it's true that rich people stay rich by being cheapskates.

She grabs a newspaper off one of the towers and starts reading. In the kitchen, I find a bin with the recycling triangle on it, full of newspapers.

Every issue is the same. No, it can't be. I hop on the back of her green couch. Behind it are four short stacks of newspapers.

They're all the same.

I can't believe it.

She must have thousands of copies of the same day's newspaper in this house. Why would anyone collect so many copies of the same paper?

On the front is a picture of a mural of a handsome man with a large forehead and the kindest eyes. All along the bottom of the mural are flowers and teddy bears and cards. Above the picture are the words "I Can't Breathe."

While she's reading and eating, I hook the red, white, and blue blanket on the back of her couch with one of my claws and tug it gently.

Her mouth full of turkey hangs open and she slowly turns her head and stares at the blanket. She starts chewing again and turns away.

I jump down and make sure she can hear the sound of my paws when I land. I hear her fork drop onto the plate. She gets up and runs around, bumping one of the taller towers in the process. It starts swaying, but she steadies it.

"Damn it all to hell. It's gonna take me forever to recenter these papers."

Once the tower is steady, she walks around the couch, looks under it, and then puts her hands on her hips.

I could do this all night.

"Call Teddy."

I hear a phone ringing from speakers in the corners of the ceiling.

"Hola."

"Buenas noches, soy Gladys."

"Ah, Señora Gladys, cómo estás?"

"Muy bien, gracias. Necesito hablar con Teddy."

"Teddy" is the name of the boy the Mustache hired to look after me.

"Hola, soy Teddy."

"Hey, kid, it's Gladys."

"Hey, Gladys, what's up?"

"Did you do what I asked you?"

"Yeah, I went to Cedars-Galilee this afternoon and saw Trench."

"How is he? What did the doctors say?"

"No change. He's still in a coma. They said he might never wake up."

"Damn it. He was my best cat-guy. You wouldn't be interested in taking his job, would you? It's easy work, and good money. All you have to do is bring me a new cat every week. I don't care where you get them. No questions asked. You wouldn't even have to wear a trench coat like he did."

"Umm, I don't think I can. I have school soon, and my mom needs me to help around the house."

"Suit yourself, kid. I'm going on vacation next week, but when I get back, I'll check in with you to see if he's out of the coma. And if you've changed your mind about being my cat-guy, let me know and the job is yours. I know your family could use the money."

"*Gracias,* Gladys."

"*De nada,* kid. *Ciao.*"

One time, when I was not a kitten but not full grown,

either, I was caught in a thunderstorm, and the water rushing down the street took my legs out from under me, and the next thing I knew, I was halfway down a storm drain, hanging on for dear life, the water rushing over me, my lungs on fire, and, for some reason I still don't understand, I started howling and biting the water, biting like it was an animal whose flesh I could take a hunk of, an animal who could feel pain and would let me go when it felt what my teeth could do.

I feel like that now.

The sun is setting. From a tower of newspapers set against the living-room window, I can see the valley below stretch flat and away until it meets the horizon, which is the color of figs.

The lights of the city in the valley come on, and the coming darkness turns everything an orange-and-pink plaid.

I thought the trees of the hills had grown legs and taken the shape of bison and elephants and saber-toothed tigers, moving up in the darkness as if they were the darkness themselves. And then I saw the shine of their bodies and knew it was the residents of the tar pits that now moved on the land.

I hadn't slept in days, so I didn't know if what I saw was a hunger dream, a dream-dream, or something else.

I don't miss sleep, if I'm honest.

I spent so many hours of every day sleeping for a hunt

that never really came. And now here I am, awake forever, and my prey right where I want them.

Are those tar animals a vision of life, or a vision of death?

When the sun disappeared, it took the residents of the tar pits with it.

The hills are quiet, and Gladys is snoring in her bedroom. If she were a bird that had pecked one of my babies, I'd pull her feathers out one at a time. And then we'd eat her while her eyes went wild and looked to the sky for help that wasn't coming.

Death is almost too good for her.

Too easy.

A cat's body is like a coil that compresses with every passing minute. At some point, the coil pops and all the energy has to go somewhere. But am I still a cat, or something else now?

Whenever the Mustache's momma would visit, she would call out in her sweet voice, "Cracker Cat!" when I would run around the room like my tail was on fire. I think it's time to introduce Gladys to Cracker Cat.

I think I have a good route. I'll start by jumping on her bed from a tower of papers, and then jump to another tower, and another, and another, in a circle around the room. It'll take her forever to restack those newspapers. Maybe she'll even have to miss a few days of work to do it, and the students will stop showing up. Or, even better, they'll call a cop or someone, anyone, to investigate the box and put a stop to all of the messed-up stuff going on in that classroom.

I'm still getting to know these new paws and legs, so I hadn't figured the newspapers would slide out from under me in large stack after stack and form a whirlwind of one day's news, or that Gladys would stumble in the dark trying to catch the papers and fall under her once-perfect towers.

Did I know that she had left a cigarette burning in the ashtray next to her bed?

I did not. It's not like me to miss something like that. No cat would miss it, in fact. Maybe I am really not a cat anymore.

If that's true, then what are the rules of this new life? How can the law of the jungle still apply if I don't have to eat anymore because I'll never experience hunger again? But what if something threatens me? Is it even possible to die again?

Halfway down the hill, I stop and look back at Gladys's house. I can't make out the house anymore, but I know where it is, because there's a feather of smoke rising high into the air, and a red tongue of fire that would lick the milk-white moon if it could.

DAY 7 QUIZ

Choose the word that best completes the sentence.

1. If you dropped a Junior Mint inside someone's body during surgery, you would ______ say something.
   a. absolutely
   b. never
   c. maybe

2. If you could choose a new career, you would become a _______.
   a. ninja
   b. monk
   c. politician

3. If the person who made you lose your job was on fire, you would ________ urinate on them to put them out.
   a. absolutely
   b. never
   c. maybe

4. I wholeheartedly ________ an animal's right to vote.
   a. applaud
   b. resist
   c. question

5. The one big regret of my adulthood is that I _______ identified as a possum.
    a. always
    b. never
    c. halfheartedly

The agave plants outside the hospital make me think of the Mustache. When I rub my lips against them, I can smell the Mustache's mouth.

He was a creature of habit if there ever was one. As soon as the first nip of fall put a chill in the air, he would change up what he ate for breakfast and set aside his boiled eggs in ice baths. If the leaves ever forgot to change to orange, I'd still know it was fall by the smells coming from the kitchen.

During the autumn months, he fries up a couple of pork sausage links in a skillet. While they're sizzling away, he cuts a few slices of goat cheese. But it isn't just any kind of goat cheese: it's been smoked.

Imagine his surprise, after eating this cheese for years, when he found out that it comes from Canary Island goats. The story goes that the Mustache's great-great-great-grandfather on his momma's side was from the Canary Islands. They came over when Texas was still Mexico.

The Majorera goat lives on Fuerteventura, the Canary Island where the cheese is made. The goats have that Old

World look, by which I mean they haven't fallen into that trap other animals have of looking like the humans who take care of them. Their faces are small triangles with soft ears and handsome eyes. Their faces are so perfect that you forget they have mouths until they let out the most beautiful baaaas. Sure, it's not songbird pretty, but the baa of a Majorera goat is a time machine. To hear it is to travel back to a time before machines or humans to run the machines, to a time when the sun kept watch over the slow business of living until the night brought sleep and dreams of water and grass and light.

I swear you can taste all this in the cheese. Anytime the Mustache cut himself some, he would always offer me a nibble. On top of the wheel of cheese is a picture of a goat in a suit and tie, smoking a pipe, and wearing a monocle. It looks like Borges, to be honest. I'd love to go up to that goat and say, "The other one, the one called Chivo, is the one things happen to. It would be an exaggeration to say that ours is a hostile relationship; I live, let myself go on living, so that Chivo may contrive his cheese, and this cheese justifies me."

Who am I kidding? The goat on that label is just a model who's probably never even heard of Borges, much less his story "Borges and I." I wonder how a goat gets into the modeling business?

That cheese was one of my favorite parts of autumn. The Mustache loved it so much that when he'd order a Royale with cheese at the movies, he'd ask for bacon, hold the tomato, onion, and cheese. He said the server always gave him a funny look until he became a regular.

After they brought him his burger, when no one was looking, he'd pull out a small baggie with a slice of smoked goat cheese in it. He'd slide that sucker into his burger, turn the burger upside down like in his experiments at home, and then wait three minutes and thirty seconds for the heat of the patty to start melting the cheese. And then voilà!

When cold weather came, the Mustache would retire his sausage-and-cheese breakfasts and out would come the oat bran. He'd make a bowl, and add pecans and raisins. And then, to tie it all together, a drizzle of agave. Before he'd close the top, he'd wipe the nozzle of the agave bottle with his finger, then let me lick it.

That agave got me so amped that I swear I could see Technicolor mice and birds in the house everywhere. Ten minutes later, I was passed out to the world.

Is that the kid getting off the bus? Yup, I think that's Teddy.

We're alone in the elevator, except for Dave Van Ronk in the speakers singing about Baltimore and crows and green rocky roads. His raspy voice is my favorite of all his voices. It reminds me of firewood crackling.

Teddy has a canvas bag with a seagull on it, but I can't make out what's inside.

He looks smaller than what I remember. Maybe dying does that—makes things look smaller, because they're farther away than you in a sense.

We could've been friends if he hadn't sold me. I know his family needs the money, but I swear, if I could push him out a window right now, I would. Who am I kidding? I could never do that. He's still somebody's baby. I guess we always are, no matter how old we get, even if our parents aren't around anymore.

There were many times when the Sculptor and Lucky Charms hardly had any money to keep us fed, and they never stole or sold animals to make ends meet. But this boy, this boy was just trying to help him momma out. I can't fault him for that, even if it cost me everything. I bet he dreams about me all the time, wonders what the end was like for me, wonders if the Mustache will buy whatever excuse he gave him or call the cops. Nah, my Mustache would never call the cops on a little kid like this. His heart is too good for something like that. He knows as well as anybody how this country makes people so desperate they do things they never would otherwise. Maybe, if I hadn't cut him, Teddy would've had second thoughts and not tricked me into that carrier and sold me to the trench-coat guy.

The hospital is busier than I thought it would be, although I've never been to a human hospital. The vet clinic was always quiet and slow. It didn't have tons of people running around like this place does.

Jeezuz, will this hallway ever end? Ugh, and what are they feeding these people? Whatever is on those trays doesn't smell like anything I'd ever eat, no matter how hungry I was. Shoot, I know the Mustache pampered me, but I'd rather eat a dirty mouse than that slop.

What's he waiting for? Why's he just standing there in front of this door that the trench-coat guy is obviously on the other side of? For Christ's sake, go in already.

Atta boy, push the door. You can do it.

Here we go, lemme just slip past his legs and—bingo!

That's a lot of machines he's hooked up to. Is that really him? I never got a good look at his face to begin with, but it kinda smells like him. It's hard to tell, with the smells of all this plastic and metal and the bleach they use to keep everything disinfected.

Let's jump up and have a look at that smile.

Oh, there's a tube in his mouth.

Good God, I can smell the broken bones in his face and his ribs. His left arm, too. Completely shattered.

He looks like a cross between a mummy and a pincushion.

I wonder how he scored a private room. He has a window with a nice view, not that he's seen it, and a TV. I wonder if they left the sound on because coma patients are supposed to be able to hear everything?

"Today we will talk with the commissioner on whether the new subway system will continue to keep traffic on the 101 light. But first, we will speak with our science expert, Dr. Rayford Clark.

"Good afternoon, Dr. Clark."

"Good afternoon, Wendy."

"Yesterday we heard about the shocking testimony of Randall 'Goose' Showalter. When his attorney asked him if he had any pre-existing conditions, he stated that he had toxoplasmosis. The defense then submitted lab results confirming the presence of toxoplasmosis in the defendant. Dr. Clark, what is toxoplasmosis?"

"Toxoplasmosis is an infection caused in humans by Toxoplasma gondii. *Under a microscope, the parasite resembles the shape of rice."*

"I see. And is this infection contagious, Doctor?"

"Yes and no. A human infected with the parasite can't pass it to another human through touch."

"How can a human come to be infected with toxoplasmosis?"

"Cats and undercooked food are the most common sources of the parasite, Wendy."

What is this dimwit talking about? Depending on what he says next, there might be a whole lot of cats in trouble in the next few days.

"You see, cats are what is known as the definitive host. A definitive host is the organism that a parasite depends upon in order to reproduce."

Well, that's just dandy. Now every yahoo between here and the Atlantic who never really took to cats is gonna see us as parasite brothels, and, what's worse, use that as an excuse to do all kinds of messed-up things to me and my kind.

"A cat will shed the dormant parasite through its feces. Animals and humans can then come in contact with the dormant parasite, like pigs, cows, birds, and mice. Once the parasite is inside you, then it can develop, which leads to toxoplasmosis."

"What sorts of preventative measures can people take, Dr. Clark?"

"Well, you can wash your hands after cleaning a litter box. People should stop eating meat rare and cook their food thoroughly. As the sheep say, rare meat is baaaaad for you."

"Excuse me, Doctor?"

"Sorry, sorry, just a little joke."

"As I mentioned, yesterday the defendant 'Goose' Show-

alter revealed that he has toxoplasmosis. In what way could his attorney make his condition relevant in this murder trial that has gripped the city?"

"Well, I can't claim to know how his attorney is planning to use a diagnosis of toxoplasmosis in his defense."

"Can you answer this question, then: what does toxoplasmosis do to the human body?"

"The effect of toxoplasmosis in the human body has been studied at length. Decades of study have shown that the parasite creates cysts in the human body. These cysts tend to collect consistently in a few areas of the body: skeletal muscle, the eyes, and the brain."

"The brain?"

"Yes, the brain. Experts are divided on whether the presence of these cysts in the human brain can change a person's personality or behavior. Studies have shown that, in a host like a mouse, the parasite reduces the inhibitions of the mouse."

"Inhibitions?"

"Yes, inhibitions. Researchers observed that the mice that were infected with Toxoplasma gondii *had absolutely no inhibitions about cats. The hypothesis is that, if the parasite could stop the mice from being afraid of cats, then a cat could eat them."*

"I don't follow, Doctor. Why would the parasite want that?"

"Because inside the stomach of a cat is the only place that the parasite can reproduce. You see, the parasite wants to go home. So that it can make more of itself."

"Thank you, Doctor. You've given us a lot to think about. I'm sure we'll speak again after Showalter is cross-examined by the prosecution."

"You're most welcome."

"Up next, five ways to inject fun into your weekend on a budget, and how many . . ."

Thank God, the kid turned off the TV. I feel sick. People will come up with any damn reason to be cruel. We cats have been around for thousands of years, living alongside humans, happy, purring our little hearts out, keeping mice away from their granaries so that humans can keep what they harvest, so they can be strong enough to build cities and, from cities, build civilizations and empires stretching from sea to sea. And what did we ask in return for all this? Love, head scratches, food, and a warm place to live. Scraps compared to what we gave the human race. What ingrates.

What's Teddy doing now? Oh, I guess it's story time for Mr. Trench Coat. I wonder what he's gonna read. Maybe a thriller or a Western novel. Or maybe it's a prayer book. Maybe he's gonna pray for him because he sure as heck needs it where he's going. Oh, a letter; this should be interesting.

Dear Bonaparte,

It's me, Teddy. I don't know if you can hear me, but I've been coming to visit you since the ambulance brought you to the hospital. I've been reading you your favorite book. I broke into your house through the bathroom window that never locks. I couldn't decide whether to bring you one of your Mustang car books to read or *Of Mice and Men,* so I brought both. I don't know if you could hear me when I was reading *Of Mice and Men.* I had to stop, because one of the nurses said that it was too sad. She said that people in comas need to hear happy things to help them wake up. I tried reading to you about Carroll Shelby and the history of the Mustang, but it was boring. Please don't hate me for not reading to you more from this book. I love it when you talk to me about Mustangs and how come they are so fast, and especially the 1969 Shelby GT350 that you say is your favorite. When you wake up, I want to hear all about the one you plan to buy when you've saved up enough money, and how you're going to drive it all the way to Alaska and start over. I have never told you this, but the part of your story where you drive to Alaska always makes me sad. You are like a big brother to me, Bonaparte, the big brother I always wanted, and not hanging out with you would make me so sad. My mom said that when you wake up she'll take us all to Randy's for donuts. I'm going to get a coconut one, you'll get a maple Long John, and my mom will say she doesn't want anything because no sweet is better than the magic bars she makes at home, haha. Don't worry about your trench coat. I picked it up while they were putting you in the ambulance and took it home. My mom washed it real good and even ironed it so that it would be fresh for you when you come home. I love you, Bonaparte. Please wake up soon. But if you need to rest longer, don't worry, I'll be here.

Love,
your friend Teddy

"Hello, kitty cat."

"Who said that? And why did it just get five degrees colder in here?"

"I did."

"Who are you?"

"I'm a friend of the man you call the Mustache."

"Wait, you can see me?"

"Of course I can, silly kitty."

"Why isn't Teddy turning around?"

"Because he can't hear or see me. Only you can."

"Are you dead?"

"In a manner of speaking."

"What does that mean?"

"I was alive once, and then I wasn't."

"Oh, great, we have a real smart aleck on our hands."

"You're too cute to talk like that."

"Look, I don't need some snot-nose girl, or whatever you are, to tell me what words I can or cannot use."

"Sorry, I didn't mean to make you angry."

"Girlie, I'm always angry."

"What could you have to be angry about?"

"I'm angry because the bastard in this bed bought me from this kid. And then he sold me to some hag in the hills who runs a school. She locked me in a box. Do you hear me? I died in that box. There was no food or water in there. And while I was rotting away in that box, students came in every day and sat around the box and felt feelings. And all for what? So they could get some stupid certificate that said that they were more in touch with their feelings than the average human."

"I'm sorry."

"That doesn't help me any."

"There's no going back. You can't go back to the life you had, only the one you have now."

"You must be some tripped-out angel or whatever you are if you think this qualifies as some kind of a life."

"Of course it's a life. You're an alebrije."

"An ale-what?"

"An alebrije, silly. Alebrijes are guides. They guide the dead, help them move around in the world."

"Now I know you're off your rocker."

"It's true. You have all the markings of one. Your fur is a bright color, and you have the traits of another animal combined with the ones you had in life. That's why you have that green fur and that cute blue armadillo shell."

"I don't want some stupid armadillo shell or green fur."

"Well, what do you want, then?"

"I want to go home. I want to lie in the Mustache's lap and feel the morning sun come in through the windows across my body and his. I want to sleep next to him, knowing that nobody in the world can hurt me as long as I'm curled up against him."

"Sounds beautiful."

"That's what I want. Can you make that happen?"

"No, I can't."

"Well, what good are you, then, if you can't do anything?"

"I never said I was powerless."

"Can you unplug Bonaparte's machines so that he stops breathing once and for all?"

"Is that really what you want?"

"You bet it is. I'd like to give him a feline necktie."

"You're funny."

"Quit laughing at me. I'm not trying to be funny."

"I can't help it. Whoever heard of a feline necktie?"

"Cats, that's who. I don't expect you'd know anything about that. My guess is you're probably one of those people who called yourself a 'dog person' when you were alive. Yeah, you have that look about you."

"I never had a chance to call myself anything, if you must know."

"Here we go with the riddles again."

"I was never born."

"Huh?"

"The Mustache and his first girlfriend were my parents."

"The Mustache, my Mustache, was your father? I don't understand."

"They were kids in college."

"No."

"Yup. It's okay. I don't blame them."

"I don't understand."

"You see, they were right to not have me. They could barely take care of themselves. And they knew this. They were babies, and while babies can have babies, babies shouldn't be raising babies."

"I'm so sorry."

"It's all right because, like I've been trying to tell you, death doesn't end anything. It's just another step on the long road of life."

"I don't follow."

"You have a lot to learn, alebrije."

"How can you not be upset that you didn't have a chance at a life?"

"But I do have a life. I have one right now."

"You can't be serious."

"Dead serious."

"That's the first time I've laughed since I don't know when."

"Since before you were kidnapped?"

"Yeah, since before I was kidnapped."

"Just because I wasn't born doesn't mean I stopped existing. For years, I've split my time between the Mustache and my momma."

"Can they see you? Like really see you with their eyes?"

"Sort of. It's more of a feeling, really. The Mustache and I have this game we like to play when he's sad and lonely. He'll sit down and then close his eyes. That's my cue to start running toward him in my cowboy gear."

"That explains the boots and hat."

"And when I get to him, he's pretending that he's a buffalo that's been stabbed and shot and is just limping around."

"Jeezuz, that's dark."

"You know our Mustache, he likes his darkness. How many times did you watch *Unforgiven* or Kurosawa or those Dirty Harry movies with him?"

"Point taken. Although lately he's been rewatching Eastwood's funny movies more, like *The Gauntlet* and the orangutan movies."

"You think *The Gauntlet* is a funny movie?"

"Well, yeah. I mean, it's not a comedy, but it has its laughs."

"Eastwood is a dark one, pussycat. Can't you see that?"

"Of course I can see that. I'm just saying he's not just all darkness. There's light stuff in there, too."

"Agree to disagree."

"So what happens when the Mustache pretends to be a buffalo?"

"Well, I pretend to chase away the buzzards that are just waiting to gobble him up."

"Sheesh, talk about dark. And you two do this often?"

"Often enough. But don't interrupt me, there's still the end."

"Sorry, sorry. Please, continue."

"So after we do that for a while, I throw my sheriff's star away, hold his big shaggy head in my hands, and then smile and jump back home in between his horns."

"I don't know what to say."

"Say you'll leave Bonaparte and Teddy here. Say you won't come back here anymore. That you'll let them try to find their way back to some sort of normal life. You're not the first or the last to ever suffer. Say that you'll leave your anger in this room."

"Not a chance, baby cakes."

"You shouldn't be up on his bed. You need to get down."

"Not before I set things right."

"How many people have to get hurt before you 'set things right'?"

"Doin' right ain't got no end."

"You sound like ole Captain Red Legs from *Josey Wales*."

"So what if I do?"

"You know he's not the hero, right? He's the psycho in that movie. He's the villain, for crying out loud!"

"You think this guy can hear me?"

"You need to get off that bed and leave him alone."

"I hope somewhere in that coma he can hear me and is quaking in his boots. Trapped in that broken body, just like he trapped my broken body in a box. Can you hear me?"

"Put your paw down. If you do this, all it'll do is rot you to the core. You think you're dead now? There's dead and then there's dead-dead. I know you have a good heart. Please, let him go and come with me."

"Where?"

"To the Mustache. I can take you to him."

"What? Are you lying to me?"

"I wouldn't do that."

"Today's your lucky day, Bonaparte. Don't go running off from this bed, now. I need to know where to find you later."

"Okay, okay, that's enough, Professor Whiskers. What's your PhD in, trash talking?"

"Maybe it is. Surely you have better jokes than that."

"Don't call me Shirley."

"Oh boy."

"Come on, we gotta get going. Let's let him enjoy the rest of his time with Teddy. Teddy really cares about him. It's the least we can do."

"Maybe the least *you* can do."

"Just have to have the last word, don't you?"

"Somebody always does. Might as well be me."

"This is gonna be a long trip. But first, we have a stop to make."

DAY 8 QUIZ

Circle the one word in each box that you most associate with Love.

again	coat
groove	water
loss	awake
wharf	oil

travel	curtain
spoon	fairly
bound	planes
lumps	growing

first	cradle
quake	drink
cheese	still
ice	so

"This is the school. Why did you bring me back here?"

"Try less talking and more listening, kitty cat."

"Our own Wendy Campbell is on the scene of an Emotional Statistics school whose entrance is surrounded by protesters. Wendy, what is the mood like at the school?"

"As you said, Sonya, protesters have gathered outside the school and are calling for its closure and an investigation into allegations that real cats are being used, and harmed, in the course. Members of the community are understandably upset. I have with me one of the students who is enrolled in the course. Sir, how long have you been taking classes here?"

"Around two weeks."

"Did you notice anything strange during your time here?"

"Yeah. I told my girlfriend that something wasn't right."

"Can you say more, sir?"

"Well, these schools say that there's supposed to be a cat inside the box. I never really thought there was one. I figured it was just a mental trick they were playing on us."

"So you have not seen inside the box—is that correct, sir?"

"Yeah, that's right. But I thought I heard a scratching sound coming from inside once."

"Has the Emotional Statistics Institute reached out to you or your classmates since the controversy began?"

"No, ma'am. Nobody has reached out to us. We have no way of knowing if the school will get shut down. And if it does, if we'll get our certificates or not."

"And what had you hoped to do with your certificate after completing the course?"

"I had planned to join my aunt Karen, working for the city to catch people who run stoplights or break the traffic laws."

"Thank you. I wish you the best of luck, sir."

"Wendy, has law enforcement issued a statement? I see some officers on the scene."

"The police chief has said his department has no comment at the moment. I believe this is the owner of the school coming down the sidewalk. Excuse me, are you Gladys Connor, the owner of this Emotional Statistics school?"

"I am."

"Would you care to comment on the allegations that your school is involved in animal cruelty?"

"No comment."

"How would you respond, then, to one of your students telling me just a few minutes ago that he thought he heard a scratching coming from inside the box at the center of your course?"

"Look, lady, my house burned down last night, and it was by the grace of God that I didn't burn up with it. I have no time to talk with you or anyone else who wants to take down the last thing I have left."

"I'm very sorry, ma'am."

"Now, get out of my way and leave me alone."

"Sonya, I spoke with an anonymous source from the police department earlier this morning who told me that the school is under investigation after they had received a tip that it might be the site of animal cruelty. As we have shared in a series of reports, while Emotional Statistics schools have been incredibly popular across the country, the recent ones that have made Schrödinger boxes the center of their curriculum have not been without controversy. In fact, if we look above us, you can see that someone in a plane wrote the words 'GO AWAY' in the sky. And not just once, but twice. Reporting live on the scene, I'm Wendy Campbell. Back to you, Sonya."

"Thanks, Wendy. In national news, a man in Georgia is set to become only the tenth parolee to attempt the controversial Egg Walk. If he can walk to Canada without breaking the egg he will be issued, then he will be granted Canadian citizenship and a chance at a new life. No past attempts by other parolees have been successful."

"So Gladys made it out of her house before it burned down, huh? That silver fox is a resilient one."

"Lucky for you, she is."

"Why lucky?"

"You don't want to become what you hate. That's a fate worse than death."

"If you say so."

"Now, come on, it's time to go."

"Where are we? What is this place?"

"Patience, pussycat."

"It smells like sweat in here. And despair. If despair can be said to have a smell."

"Oh, it can. And it does."

"Who is this man?"

"He's an attorney. A public defender, to be exact."

"Is he assigned to Bonaparte's case?"

"Not exactly."

"What does that mean?"

"If that man wasn't in a coma, then this attorney probably wouldn't be here. Or if by chance he still did end up in this room, then he'd be waiting for someone different."

"Enough with the double-talk already. Can you just spill it? Why is he here, and more importantly, why did you bring me here?"

"Listen. Do you hear that?"

"I hear a lot of things. The unbearable bang of iron on iron, people shouting, keys jingling. Buzzers buzzing. Paint peeling."

"The only thing missing is a partridge cooing in a pear tree."

"Oh boy."

"Focus on the hallway outside this door. Listen for feet. Do you hear that?"

"I do. Is that . . . ? Is that the Mustache's shuffle? Is that him?"

"It is, kitty cat."

"I'd know that uneven shuffle anywhere. I always hoped he'd get that crooked pelvis checked out. I just didn't have any way to tell him that it was off kilter."

"I know."

"Wait—if he's here, he's in jail. Why is he in jail?"

"Just watch and listen. Here he is now."

"Good morning."

" 'Morning."

"Are you eating?"

"Yessir. Some."

"The food's not great, but I've been told by some clients that it's better than it used to be."

"I've had better. And worse."

"Are you able to sleep? Oftentimes, people who are in jail for the first time have trouble sleeping."

"I'm not sleeping much."

"Is the bed too hard? That's what first-time clients say."

"No, I like a firm bed. It's my mind. I can't turn it off. I just keep thinking and thinking."

"That's understandable. What are you thinking about?"

"How I got here. One day, I'm living my life, and while it wasn't perfect, it was okay, and then the next, I'm in here and charged with attempted murder."

"This country is full of people who don't understand just how fragile their freedom is."

"Yeah, I get that now."

"Well, have you given any more thought to what I proposed?"

"I don't want to talk to a shrink. I'm not crazy."

"I'm not saying you're crazy, but if I'm going to pursue a plea of temporary insanity, then we're going to need an expert to testify that during the attack you had temporarily lost your ability to tell right from wrong."

"But what I did felt right. I wanted to kill that man. It's only by the grace of God that I didn't."

"Please, don't ever repeat that to anyone but me."

"I may not be a lawyer, but I'm not dumb."

"Are you sure about that? Look, I don't know you. You seem like a decent guy. My job is to help you not spend the rest of your life in prison. But in order to do that job, I need you to help me, not work against me."

"I'm sorry. Do you know what happens to prisoners who are certified mentally ill?"

"I've heard the stories."

"They're not just stories. There aren't enough beds, so the overflow of mentally ill prisoners are chained to chairs in the intake center. For days."

"I have friends at the ACLU who are looking into it."

"Well, while they look into it, these men are chained to these chairs, and sometimes the guards don't even let them get up to use the restroom, so they just end up pissing and shitting themselves. What exactly do you think pissing and shitting yourself is going to do for someone's mental health? Huh? I can tell you, it ain't good. Correctional facilities don't correct anything."

"I know things aren't easy. But you have to hang in there. Just please give the temporary insanity plea some more thought. Think about the time it could save you in the future."

"Look, I messed up. I let my anger get the better of me, and I almost killed someone because of it. It wouldn't feel right if I got off free because I pretended to be crazy."

"You're not . . ."

"Just listen. Please."

"Okay."

"I deserve to be punished. I can't control what that punishment will look like, but what I can control is what I do from this point forward. It has to start with taking responsibility for what I did. Did you talk to the DA about a plea deal?"

"I did. You're not going to like it."

"What are the terms?"

"Twenty-five to life. With the possibility of parole after fifteen."

"Jesus."

"This is if you plead guilty and write a statement of apology to the victim and his family."

"Is there any way to shorten it? Will the DA consider a lesser sentence if you ask her?"

"I can try, but I doubt it. There is one thing that could shorten how much time you spend behind bars."

"What's that?"

"The Egg Walk."

"The Egg Walk? You can't be serious. Nobody has ever successfully done it, have they?"

"Not yet. Quite a few people have tried, though. Nine, to be exact."

"Jeezuz, has it really come to that?"

"Desperate times. You think things are bad now, just wait until you're in a prison. Becoming a number changes you. Losing your freedom changes you. Hell, even losing the ability to use the toilet in private changes you. You're getting a taste of it now, and I know it's unpleasant, but I won't BS you, it gets worse. A lot worse."

"What *is* the Egg Walk? How does it work?"

"Twenty years ago, Mexico, the US, and Canada ratified the North American Accords. Part of those accords detailed an early-release program whereby a prisoner serving a sentence of twenty-five years or more could, after five years, with good behavior, attempt to walk to one of the other countries. The country chosen would be the one farthest away from the prison."

"So Canada?"

"Yes. And upon the prisoner's release, they are given an egg with their inmate number on it. If the prisoner makes it to the border of the other country, Canada in your case, without breaking the egg, and without having hitched a ride with anyone, then they are free to live their lives as they choose. It's a second chance."

"What if the egg breaks? Or if I hop a train for part of the trip?"

"Then the belt around your waist will notify the authorities monitoring you, and you'll be picked up within a few hours."

"Is that it? They'd just take me back to prison?"

"Sort of. You'd be placed on death row."

"Boy, you really know how to sell this program."

"I'm just being honest."

"What about food and shelter?"

"People are allowed to give you food, and fresh clothes, but you have to stay outside."

"Well, at least that's something."

"I'm going to ask you one last time: are you sure you want me to enter a plea of guilty on your behalf?"

"Yeah, let's do it. The sooner my clock starts, the sooner I can get to five years and start making my way up to Canada. I always wanted to see Portland and Seattle. And, anyhow, a friend once told me how beautiful Victoria is. He said that as soon as you cross that border, the air is fresher, the trees are greener, and the bald eagles . . . the bald eagles are everywhere in the sky, just turning and turning, like giant, beautiful kites."

"That sounds nice."

"Yeah."

"All right, you take care of yourself. Get some sleep, and I'll be in touch."

"Yessir. Thank you."

Flowers and flowers and flowers all over me, so many that I look like an orange bouquet in an orange bowl.

"You can't stay here forever."

"How the heck did you get here? Did you follow me here?"

"I am of here, kitty cat."

"Did you always talk like that?"

"Talk like what?"

"Like you forgot what century this is."

"Well, if you want to get technical about it, I'm not from any century."

"I guess you have a point. So you're just a regular old little flower girl, aren't you?"

"More than you know. I am the marriage of life and death, the marriage of here and there, the marriage of yesterday and tomorrow."

"Well, that sounds fancy. What's your name?"

"I don't have one."

"Are you pulling my leg?"

"Not at all."

"Doesn't that bother you, not having a name?"

"I never gave it much thought."

"You're a weird one."

"Says the blue-green catadillo."

"Touché."

"The Mustache and my momma never gave me a name. Which is all right. Besides, names are important in the world they live in. Here, in the in-between, not so much."

"Who did the Mustache put in a coma?"

"I think you know the answer to that."

"No. It can't be."

"Why not?"

"He's the most gentle person I've ever known."

"Love will make people do crazy things."

"Love?"

"Come on, you know how much he loves you. And when he found out that the neighbor kid he'd hired to watch you had sold you, well, he kinda did go out of his mind in a way."

"He didn't hurt Teddy, did he?"

"No. A part of him probably wanted to, but he could never hurt a child."

"All this time I thought he had forgotten about me. I didn't know he was trapped in a box, too."

"He's a good man."

"I want to go home."

"Your wish is my command."

. . .

This is my bed. That's my water bowl. Ugh, no one's changed my litter box since I was kidnapped.

The sun is coming in through the windows and splashing across my spot on the sofa, only there's no one here to purr or to let that light warm their belly.

I don't feel warm or cold anymore. I just am.

I don't belong here anymore.

"Cowgirl, are you there?"

"I'm here."

"How far back can I travel in time? Can I see the Mustache when he was a boy?"

"No. You can't go back any further than the day of your birth."

"That seems dumb. And I think you mean 'farther.' "

"No, it's 'further.' "

"I'm a cat, sort of, at least I was a cat, and I think I would know what 'farther' means."

" 'Farther' refers to the physical distance between one thing and another. 'Further' refers to the figurative distance between two things. For example, your understanding of what 'farther' means could not be further from the truth."

"You're just a regular joke-factory, aren't you?"

"I do all right."

"Let's get out of here."

"Okay. Where do you wanna go?"

"Surprise me."

. . .

"Where are we?"

"Just keep your eyes on that restaurant, the one with the bay window, and perk those feline ears."

I've never been in that restaurant, but I recognize the smell. I'd know the smell of those heirloom tomatoes anywhere. Those tomatoes were used to make the sauce of the spaghetti and meatballs the Mustache would bring home for dinner every Sunday. He said those tomatoes were fine enough to eat like apples, unlike the nasty Romas that taste like dirty water when you bite into them.

I never knew he was picking up our Sunday dinners from this place.

"Oh, that's him in the window! Who's that woman he's with?"

"She's the woman he was dating the day he adopted you."

"I had no idea."

"That's because they broke up just after this."

"Why are they sitting in that window?"

"It's the exit interview. At fancy restaurants, before a customer can leave, they have to sit in the bay window for their exit interview."

"What will they think up next?"

"Restaurants use it as a way to be more sensitive to the needs of their clientele. Their assumption is that the customer's impressions of the meal and the service will be freshest just after they are done. It makes sense."

"But they're just sitting there in silence."

"That's because you didn't get to see how the meal went. Try to hear them. I know there's glass and we're on this busy sidewalk, but you're an alebrije, you're capable of much more than you think."

"Did she just suggest to my Mustache that she will assume that whatever he says and does is wrong from now on?"

"Yeah."

"No wonder he ended things. It was him who ended things, right?"

"It was. And then he went to the shelter and found you, Miss Cranky Pants."

"He never told me any of this. Or said anything about her."

"He had no reason to."

"He's never going to make it in prison. He was putting on a brave face while talking to his attorney, but that's all it was, a face."

"Maybe he's tougher than you think?"

"No, I think I know him pretty well. He's the kindest person I've ever met."

"I'd say I know him pretty well, too. And I've known him longer."

"I'm sorry, I didn't mean any disrespect."

"It's okay."

"It's not that I think he can't survive. I know he can

survive. What I meant when I said that he won't make it in prison is that the person he is, the kind, gentle, loving man I've known, that man is going to have to go somewhere deep inside of himself, that man will have to disappear. And in that man's place, a different man, a tougher man will have to show up, one who is willing to do what it takes in order to survive in a dangerous place, a place that is meant to strip you of your humanity."

"You don't think he can hold on until the five years are up and then he can try the Egg Walk?"

"With his bum pelvis, he wouldn't even make it halfway to Oregon. What's more, I don't know how many eggs you've handled in the spirit world, but walking a thousand miles without breaking one is nearly impossible. And the smell after a few days would be unbearable."

"All good points."

"Take me to him."

"Are you sure?"

"A hundred percent. I have to save him."

"What's your plan?"

"I'll figure it out as I go along."

"You'll figure it out?"

"Yeah."

"No offense, kitty cat, but you don't look like you have a lot of experience breaking anyone out of jail."

"But do you know what I do have? A can-do attitude, and when I make my mind up about something, look out.

In the immortal words of Bruce Willis, I'm "just the fly in the ointment, Hans, the monkey in the wrench, the pain in the ass.' "

"Well, I hope you're right. I can take you to the jail, but I can't go with you."

"Why in the world not?"

"Because I can't see him like that. It's one thing when your papa pretends to be a shaggy buffalo that's been stabbed and shot, and it's another when it's not pretend anymore because life is currently kicking the shit out of him, pardon my French."

"I get it. I do."

"I wish you luck, sweet kitty."

"Thanks. I'm gonna need it."

DAY 9 QUIZ

Circle the one word in each box that you most associate with the Future.

again	coat
groove	water
loss	awake
wharf	oil

travel	curtain
spoon	fairly
bound	planes
lumps	growing

first	cradle
quake	drink
cheese	still
ice	so

"Are you there, Cowgirl?" I guess she meant it when she said she wouldn't be coming.

I've walked around this jail at least ten times. It looks like the ugliest multilayer cake you've ever seen. If cakes were made out of stone.

I can see a way out through the back if I can keep my focus and short-circuit the locking mechanism of the doors. I wish I could just wrap the Mustache up into a ball with me so we could blip out of here to the flower world. Or anywhere but here, really.

Home would be nice. If only we could go back there and just resume our lives as they were before he went to visit his mother.

Okay, here goes nothing.

What in the world is the Mustache's cellmate, Nate, babbling about? Whoa, how did I know his name was Nate? Maybe being an alebrije comes with a sixth sense? Or a seventh or eighth sense?

"Words. I have all the best words, you know. Just the

absolute best. You've never seen words as good as my words."

"I know you do, Nate."

"If you need some new words, you let me know. Don't ask anyone else, because no one else's words are going to be better than mine."

"I know. They're pretty good words."

What is the Mustache doing with all these lists of words?

"It's been a long time since someone made a new thesaurus, Nate. This project will be a genuine contribution to society. It has to be."

"Which word are you working on right now?"

"The word 'maybe.' People don't give that word a lot of thought, but it's a mighty powerful word."

"Can I see what you have so far?"

"Of course. Here, take a look."

MAYBE
possible
by chance
hope
could be
perhaps
love
adventure
sure

practically
likely
conceivably
child
might
dark clouds
crystal ball
full moon
credible
kindness

"That's a mighty fine list."

"Thanks, Nate. I think it's off to a good start. Have you thought about that conversation we had? About the prisons?"

"I have friends in a few of them. I reached out to my people, and they said you won't be safe for long in any of them."

"Why the heck not?"

"Because that guy you killed was connected. He has people in a lot of the prisons. That certificate program he was supplying the cats with is used by a lot of ex-cons. It looks good if they can do the class and get a certificate that says they're more in touch with their feelings. It makes parole officers look good, and future employers less uneasy about hiring a felon. You killing the guy fucks things up a bit."

"I didn't kill him, Nate."

"Well, can he talk? Can he feed himself?"

"No."

"Well then, he might as well be dead. And dead is what I hear you're gonna be after you plead out and get transferred."

"Fuck, fuck, fuck."

"You're never gonna make it to that Egg Walk, brother. I'm sorry."

"You're not going to kill me, are you?"

"Me? Nah, nobody sent me to kill you. I'm here because I fell asleep driving my rig and ran into a parked car. Shit, man, I don't even live in this crazy city."

"Where are you from?"

"Central Valley."

"You got anyone? Any little Nates running around?"

"Yeah. My old lady's back home. We got two kids. She hasn't told them yet that their old man is locked up. I told her I wanted to do it. Reminded her that I got the best words. Best words you ever did see."

"How'd she take it?"

"She told me to sort my shit out and get home before next week, because she was gonna have to tell the kids something by then. I told her not to, that they're used to work taking me out of town for long stretches. But she has a mind of her own, so I need to figure all this out as soon as possible. I don't want my kids to think of me as a jailbird. Or, worse, to have the other kids in school find out and then tease them about it. Kids can be cruel little fuckers. You got any kids?"

"Nope. I never found the right person I wanted to have them with."

"Who said you need the right person?"

"Ha! Well, it certainly doesn't hurt."

"Truer words were never spoken. Say, what are the next words you're going to make entries for?"

" 'Night,' 'under,' 'all,' 'lamp.' "

"Those are pretty good ones."

"Thanks, Nate."

"What made you choose those?"

"They're all in this poem I love."

"No shit. I like poems, too. You ever heard of this poem called "Samurai Song"? It's by a poet named Pinsky from Jersey."

"Can't say that I have. How's it go?"

"When I had no roof I made
Audacity my roof. When I had
No supper my eyes dined."

"Wow, that's incredible. Is that the whole thing?"

"That's all I can remember."

"I really love that poem. I'll have to memorize it, even though I've never really had the memory for something like that. I can remember a face forever, but a string of words—well, that's another story."

"Well, this is a good poem to start with. But you said you were drawing your words from a poem?"

"Oh yeah. It's called 'Maybe All This' and it's by a Polish poet. Do you know any Polish poets, Nate? Her name is Wisława Szymborska."

"Man, that's a mouthful."

"It is, it is. I only have the first few lines memorized. It goes like this.

"Maybe all this
is happening in some lab?
Under one lamp by day
and billions by night?"

"I don't get it, but it sounds nice."

"You'd probably have to read the whole thing for it to make any sense."

"Yeah, poetry is like that."

"LIGHTS OUT!"

"Guess we better turn in. Tomorrow's another day."

" 'Night, Nate."

I could watch my Mustache sleep for a thousand days and nights. Oh, my sweet, sweet baby, how did you end up in this place? You don't belong here. You belong at home with me, only home isn't how we left it anymore, is it? Everything's changed. You'd probably be terrified if you saw me. Might not even want to scratch my head or let me sit in your lap. And I wouldn't blame you. Who could ever love a monster like me?

What's Nate doing awake? And what's that in his hand? That's no samurai, but it'll do the trick just as well. His lips are moving, and though I'm no lip reader, I can hear even the smallest whisper better, now that I'm an alebrije.

"They didn't say I had to kill him today. Tomorrow should be just as good. Fuck, I wish he wasn't such a nice guy. And I wish they hadn't told me to make it messy. But orders are orders."

I can feel my blue shell trying to stretch out and wrap me up. I can't let it. I can't let my fear make me run. I can do something. I have to do something.

I could kill Nate. No, they'd just send another Nate, whoever they are, if he didn't get the job done. The world is full of Nates ready to say "How high?" when someone says jump.

There's only one thing to do.

I can't.

But I have to. There's no other way. As soon as Nate is back asleep, I have to do it.

Nate can snore in this jail cell because he knows no one was sent in here to kill him. He doesn't have a target on his back. Yet. Look at him, sleeping there like a big baby, without a care in the world, with his stupid orange hair. I could open him like a ripe melon. The world would be better for it, too. No, I'll let evil take care of evil.

I never believed in that word before. It's a curious word. Rearrange the letters and you land on "live." But "vile" is also in there, too. And so is "veil."

I can't count how many times I've curled up beside my Mustache like this, right between his neck and his shoulder. I can feel his soft breath run down the length of my back. How am I supposed to do this?

I can't.

But I have to.

Stretched across his neck like this, I bet from a distance I would look like a blue scarf with green ends.

No, I love him too much.

There has to be another way.

I remember the next day Nate wiping the sleep from his eyes and mumbling that today was going to be the day.

I remember he fixed his face for malice, and when he stood up, I stretched right across his foot and felt him fall through the air and land on his face against the concrete floor.

I remember he bounced up and shouted that his nose was broken and pounded the floor with one hand and kicked his feet.

I remember the Mustache rushing to him and holding

one of his towels against Nate's nose and calling for help, which came and took Nate to the infirmary.

I remember watching Nate in the infirmary and hearing the crack of his nose when the doctor reset it and flicking my tail and wondering what goes on in the mind of someone who is asked to kill someone else and who says, "Yes, I can do that," and then goes ahead and tries to do it.

I remember Nate returning to the cell with a bandage on his nose and the smile of my sweet, dear Mustache when he saw the man he thought was the only friend he had left in the world, and what could I say if I could have said anything about anything that wasn't the truth, a thing that not even I would believe if I wasn't living it.

I remember Nate talking on the phone with his family back home, and how I followed him everywhere, including the one time he was mumbling about how the shower, yes, the shower was when he would finally do it, and he said this in the library with no one around in a voice as light as dust.

I remember how slow his eyes blinked, as if they were blinking for the first time in their lives, when I flipped the page of the magazine he was reading.

I remember how he crossed himself not once but twice, and thinking that his being a man of faith could be useful.

I remember how he tried to kill the Mustache again, and how, before the Mustache could even know, Nate knew I was there, because I had become the slowly widening crack in his understanding of what reality was and what reality could be.

I remember that night I entered Nate's dreams like a tidal wave of orange flowers, and how he tried to swim to a shore he could not see.

I remember tossing Nate on a beach of black sand and waiting for him to see the hump of my shell moving above the waters far out, waiting for him to be properly worried before I began moving slowly toward the shore.

I remember the water dripping off of me as I sank one heavy green foot after another on the beach and walked toward him.

I remember him scuttling backward like a crab that I could crack and devour if I was the type to devour crabs, except I was now beyond food of the water and the air and the earth because I now belonged to none of them, just as I belonged to all of them.

I remember telling him that his broken nose, the flipped page, every single time he thought his imagination was getting the better of him, was, in fact, me getting the better of him.

I remember telling him that I was a demon who owned the soul of his cellmate, and that if he harmed him I would come for him, but not stop there, because I would also find his family in the Valley and do the worst things he could imagine to them.

I remember the way his mouth tightened when I told

him he had choices to make when he woke up, and that only one of them did not lead to his death.

I remember he crossed himself and closed his eyes and said, *Wake up, wake up, wake up,* over and over, until it became like a kind of prayer.

I remember how, before I let him slip from this dream and back to the cold of his cell, I nuzzled his ear and licked the top of it as I said, *What's mine is mine,* and then bit off a tiny bit of the top of his ear.

I remember he screamed and I said, *This is just a reminder of the evening. Something so that you'll know you were here,* because that's what the demon in *The Golden Child* said to Eddie Murphy when he cut his forearm in a dream.

I remember when Nate woke up and felt the missing part of his ear, and how so many cats I had known had woken up and found parts of their ears clipped after they had been fixed and vaccinated and returned to the streets.

I remember hearing Nate explain during visiting hours to someone that the hit needed to be called off, because there was a witch or a demon or something equally as bad that had a hold of the man he was supposed to kill, the man who was obsessed with the word "maybe."

I remember sighing like I hadn't sighed in a long time.

DAY 10: FINAL QUIZ

Circle the one word in each box that you most associate with the word Mercy.

again	coat
groove	water
loss	awake
wharf	oil

travel	curtain
spoon	fairly
bound	planes
lumps	growing

first	cradle
quake	drink
cheese	still
ice	so

" 'Morning, Teddy."

"Good morning, Ms. Taylor."

"I never get tired of the way those sliding doors whoosh your hair up."

"It's so quiet at the hospital today."

"Mhmmm, I've been at my desk all morning, and not a single soul has asked me how to find the gift shop or where the cafeteria is. One man did think this was the entrance to the ER, but that's about it. You bring anything new to read to your friend?"

"No, still working on *Bless Me, Ultima.*"

"I don't know that one."

"My mom told me to go slow because it has a lot of words. I hope Bonaparte is liking it."

"Tell him I said hi."

"I will! See ya. Hold the elevator!"

"Hey, Bonaparte."

Beep.

"How are you feeling today? I'm good."

Beep.

"Ms. Taylor at the information desk downstairs told me to say hi to you. I think you'd like her. She's pretty nice. My mom says hi, too."

Beep.

"She told me to check your eyelids when I got here, because she said you're probably just faking so that you can get the royal treatment. I told her no way I was gonna lift your eyelids! But in case you are awake and pretending, I brought some of my mom's special granola, so if you wake up, I'll share it with you. What do you think? You want some?"

Beep.

"Gotcha. More granola for me, then. Okay, let's see, where did I leave off? Chapter Diez.

"'The summer came and burned me brown with its energy, and the llano and the river filled me with their beauty. The story of the golden carp continued to haunt my dreams.'

"Speaking of dreams, I had this weird one last night, Bonaparte. I dreamed that I was at this ranch. I think in the dream I lived there, because I knew where everything was. There was a corral, and in the middle of it was a sawhorse painted black and white, like a pinto. Someone had painted blue eyes on it, and there was fire coming out of the nose. But that's not all."

Beep.

"There was this little girl who was dressed like a cowboy. She had on chaps and a vest and a big hat. She was swinging this lasso and using it to rope the head of the sawhorse. The head was a broken mop that had been nailed on one end. Did I mention that?"

Beep.

"So, this little girl, she was cute. She was, like, my age, only she didn't look like any of the girls in my grade. There was something about her that made me think she was older. Or maybe she wasn't even a little girl at all, just some ghost pretending to be one, ya know?"

Beep.

"I asked my mom what she thought it meant. She said it was probably the burritos we had for dinner. She said she told me not to put so much cheese on mine. What do you think it means?"

"New patient coming in. Coming through."

"Oh, hey, Nurse Yvonne."

"Hi, Teddy. We have a new roommate for Bonaparte today. This is Frank. And that's his aunt Karen and his girlfriend . . . I'm sorry, what was your name again?"

"My name is Ali."

"Yes, Ali, sorry. I'm just gonna get Frank's bed set up, and then I'll be out of your hair."

"My name is Teddy. This is Bonaparte."

"Hi, Teddy, I'm Frank's girlfriend. It's nice to meet you. Were you reading something? We didn't mean to interrupt you."

"Oh yeah, I was just reading a book to my friend."

"Aunt Karen, why are you giving me that look? It wasn't my fault."

"I should've never agreed to train you, Frankie."

"But I got my certificate!"

"Yeah, and then the school that gave it to you closed down the following week."

"Hey, that's not my fault."

"It's not your fault. It's mine. First off, you're my kin. That right there is reason alone to not have trained you. But here we are in the hospital, with you all banged up on your first week of work."

"Teddy . . ."

"Bonaparte! Oh my God, you're awake! I can't believe it! Somebody call the nurse!"

"Teddy . . . more . . ."

"More? I can barely hear you, Bonaparte. More what?"

"More . . . burritos."

"Burritos?"

"The dream . . . the cowgirl."

"Ooooooh."

"Maybe the dream means you should eat more burritos."

Flowers.

I don't know how long I was in the orange world after I left the Mustache safe at the jail. It was like sleep but not sleep. I was neither happy nor sad. I left because I wanted to feel happy again.

I remember I followed the Mustache from the jail to prison, and I slept beside his bed for years.

I remember his mustache going from the color of midnight, to midnight with shooting stars.

I remember the sound of his breath.

I remember the day he was released early for good behavior.

I remember the mountains he moved to in search of a new life.

I remember love found him under the shadow of an aspen.

. . .

I remember a boy and a girl followed not long after.

I remember he kept a photo of me and what I used to look like framed on his nightstand.

I remember the moment it was time to leave him, because he now had his life and it was time to find mine.

I remember when I came to this barn. I didn't know the Italian meadows would stretch out so far. I didn't know that watching a cow be asked for its milk, and then give it, could be a type of heaven.

I remember running on water.

I remember Key lime pie.

I remember windows.

I remember birds that were my friends.

I remember breakfast.

I remember apples.

I remember meows.

I remember horses and their giant teeth.

. . .

I remember alleyways.

I remember empty bellies and bellies filled to bursting.

I remember tripas frying in golden oil.

I remember salt.

I remember tacos.

I remember the deep blue sea.

I remember toes.

I remember the chubby legs of children.

I remember fog.

I remember Christmas trees.

I remember ornaments shaped like fish.

I remember hens and their chicks.

I remember learning the trumpet a rooster blew every morning.

. . .

I remember shadows.

I remember mirrors.

I remember my babies.

I remember purrs.

I remember trash cans and their symphony of smells.

I remember furniture.

I remember mice.

I remember balloons.

I remember boots and a certain puss who wore them.

I remember midnight.

I remember honeycombs.

I remember calendars of kittens.

I remember crowds.

I remember every song I ever heard.

. . .

I remember Queequeg.

I remember narwhals.

I remember mothers.

I remember questions I never asked.

I remember lullabies.

I remember roads of dirt and roads of water.

I remember grass.

I remember blueberries bursting.

I remember dense ivy.

I remember pear trees.

I remember a dog eating the pears.

I remember the sweetness of his farts.

I remember hunger.

I remember sneezes.

. . .

I remember trains.

I remember cherry pies.

I remember galoshes.

I remember corduroy.

I remember licking my mother's fur.

I remember time.

I remember Joseph Cornell.

I remember lobsters.

I remember the ballet.

I remember the secrets of lobster ballerinas.

I remember sweat.

I remember snow.

I remember graveyards.

I remember sunning on headstones.

. . .

I remember families in mourning gathered like tuxedo cats.

I remember cars that hiss.

I remember men with shovels.

I remember smelling this hay that is wet from the kiss of the damp mornings here.

I remember the large, almost sad eyes of these cows.

I remember the long and gentle fingers of the Mustache on my head.

I remember him finding me here as if it was yesterday after he said goodbye to a long and full life.

I remember he crossed his legs when he sat on the ground next to me.

I remember the cows when he asked me, “Is this heaven?”

I remember they kept chewing the seconds and minutes and hours, in no rush.

I remember wondering, have I ever been happier?

Not that I can remember.

ACKNOWLEDGMENTS

Thank you to the National Endowment for the Arts for awarding a fellowship in prose to this poet who had a story to tell, even though I still had no idea how to tell it. While that award gave me the time to write this book, the Civitella Ranieri Foundation gave me the space to begin writing it among a wonderful, nurturing group of amazing artists. Big thanks to Rice University and my colleagues for all your support.

So much gratitude to my wonderful agent Dan Mandel for taking a chance on me, and to Courtney Zoffness for connecting us and for all your moral support. Where do I even begin to thank my editor Deborah Garrison? You saw what this book could be and over many drafts helped me find my way to the best version of this story, always encouraging me to trust my vision, while also helping me expand it. Endless thanks to the brilliant Lisa Lucas for believing in this novel and for making a home for it at Pantheon.

Sunil Yapa, T. Bambrick, Josh Lopez, Hasanthika Sirisena, a crackerjack squad of early readers if there ever was one. Each of you helped me puzzle my way through different parts of the book. Erin Evans, there's no way to thank you enough for inspiring me on and off the page. The way you believe in me makes me feel ten feet tall and like I could write anything. Thank you for always dreaming with me in our own purrfect way, haha.

Last, but not least, I dedicate this book to Lindsey, my tortie cat whose sass and courage and spirit I channeled into this book. It was truly a gift to be your family for twenty years.

A NOTE ABOUT THE AUTHOR

TOMÁS Q. MORÍN is the author of the memoirs *Let Me Count the Ways,* winner of the 2023 Vulgar Geniuses Award for Nonfiction, and *Where Are You From: Letters to My Son,* as well as the poetry collections *Machete, Patient Zero,* and *A Larger Country.* He is coeditor, with Mari L'Esperance, of the anthology *Coming Close: Forty Essays on Philip Levine,* and a translator of *The Heights of Macchu Picchu* by Pablo Neruda. He is a fellow of the Guggenheim Foundation and the National Endowment for the Arts.

A NOTE ABOUT THE TYPE

This book was set in Arno, a typeface designed by Adobe principal designer Robert Slimbach in 2007. Its namesake is the Arno River, which flows through Florence, the city at the heart of the Italian Renaissance. Inspired by the humanist letterforms of the fifteenth and sixteenth centuries, Slimbach designed Arno with the vitality and readability of Venetian and Aldine book typefaces in mind.

Composed by North Market Street Graphics,
Lancaster, Pennsylvania

Designed by Marisa Nakasone